THE FORCE

Follow the bestsel̲  **RS**

HEIRS OF THE FORCE

In the jungle outside the academy, the twins make a startling discovery—the remains of a crashed TIE fighter. The original pilot, an Imperial trooper, has been living wild in the jungles since his crash. Waiting for a chance to return to duty . . .

SHADOW ACADEMY

Thanks to the dark Jedi Brakiss—Luke Skywalker's former student—the dark side of the Force has a new training ground. The Shadow Academy!

THE LOST ONES

Jacen and Jaina could lose an old and dear friend. Zekk is wild and free in the underground mazes of Coruscant . . . and a perfect candidate for the Shadow Academy!

LIGHTSABERS

Luke Skywalker has come to a grim conclusion. The Shadow Academy has become very powerful, and the New Republic needs all the warriors it can muster. It is time for the young Jedi Knights to build their weapons . . .

And now, the Young Jedi Knights' most exciting adventure:

DARKEST KNIGHT

This book also contains a special sneak preview of the next *Star Wars: Young Jedi Knights* adventure:

JEDI UNDER SIEGE

ABOUT THE AUTHORS

KEVIN J. ANDERSON and his wife, **REBECCA MOESTA**, have been involved in many STAR WARS projects. Together, they are writing the eleven volumes of the YOUNG JEDI KNIGHTS saga for young adults, as well as creating the JUNIOR JEDI KNIGHTS series for younger readers. Rebecca Moesta is also writing the second trilogy of JUNIOR JEDI KNIGHTS adventures.

Kevin J. Anderson is also the author of the STAR WARS: JEDI ACADEMY trilogy, the novel *Darksaber*, and the comic series THE SITH WAR for Dark Horse comics. His young adult fantasy novel, *Born of Elven Blood*, written with John Betancourt, was published in 1995 by Atheneum. He has edited several STAR WARS anthologies, including *Tales from the Mos Eisley Cantina*, in which Rebecca Moesta has a story, and *Tales from Jabba's Palace*.

STAR
YOUNG JEDI KNIGHTS
WARS®
DARKEST KNIGHT

KEVIN J. ANDERSON
and REBECCA MOESTA

BOULEVARD BOOKS, NEW YORK

STAR WARS: YOUNG JEDI KNIGHTS
DARKEST KNIGHT

A Boulevard Book / published by arrangement with
Lucasfilm Ltd.

PRINTING HISTORY
Boulevard edition / June 1996

The Putnam Berkley World Wide Web site address is
http://www.berkley.com

ISBN: 1-57297-129-0

BOULEVARD
Boulevard Books are published by The Berkley Publishing Group,
200 Madison Avenue, New York, New York 10016.
BOULEVARD and its logo are trademarks
belonging to Berkley Publishing Corporation.

PRINTED IN THE UNITED STATES OF AMERICA

10 9 8 7 6 5 4 3 2 1

To Skip Shayotovich,
whose enthusiasm knows no bounds

acknowledgments

The usual round of thanks to Lillie E. Mitchell and her fast fingers for transcribing our dictation; Lucy Autrey Wilson, Sue Rostoni, and Allan Kausch at Lucasfilm for their helpful suggestions; Ginjer Buchanan at Berkley/Boulevard for her whole-hearted support and encouragement; and Jonathan MacGregor Cowan for being our test reader and brainstormer.

STAR
YOUNG JEDI KNIGHTS
WARS.

DARKEST KNIGHT

1

THE MASSASSI TREES that towered over Yavin 4's jungles were smaller than the enormous wroshyr trees on the Wookiee homeworld, but Lowbacca considered them to be the next best thing. Especially when he needed to be alone, in a place where he could sort out his thoughts.

As twilight descended on the jungle moon with a blanket of colors deepening in hue, Lowie ascended one of the thickest, tallest trees in the vicinity of the Great Temple, the site of Luke Skywalker's Jedi academy. With his retractable Wookiee claws and muscular arms, he grabbed on to branches and hauled his lanky body up one level after another, increasing the distance between himself and the ground. It seemed that if he kept climbing, he might almost be able to reach the stars . . . and be closer to home.

Stopping to rest momentarily, Lowie reached out to grasp a hairy green vine, tugged to make

1

sure it would hold his weight, then used it to climb even higher. He had to reach the top. The top was the best place.

The best place to think.

It had been a long time since he had been back to the Wookiee world of Kashyyyk. He hadn't seen his immediate family since departing for Yavin 4 to begin training as a Jedi Knight. Although Lowie loved tinkering with computers—as did his sister and his parents—he wanted more than anything to make use of his special, undefinable talent, a potential for using the Force that few Wookiees in his family line had ever exhibited.

When Lowie first arrived at the Jedi academy, uncertain and alone, his uncle Chewbacca had given him a T-23 skyhopper as a gift, so he could cruise far out into the jungle. Sometimes he brought his friends Jacen and Jaina and Tenel Ka. At other times, though, he just needed to be by himself, far from everyone. And this was one of those times.

He missed his family very much, especially his younger sister Sirrakuk. A very dangerous time in her life was fast approaching. . . .

With a great heave, Lowie used one long arm to draw his body up to a leafy nest of branches, where he disturbed a shrieking horde of the voracious tree rodents called stintarils. Stintarils normally ate anything in sight, anything that moved—but when Lowie treated them to his best Wookiee roar, the chittering rodents scampered away through the trees, kicking up clouds of broken twigs and leaves.

At last, surrounded by the dimming colors of dusk, Lowie parted the final blanket of leaves overhead. He braced his broad, flat feet on a sturdy branch, pushed his head above the treetops, and stood there, drinking in the distance. He looked across the sprawling jungle that spread all around him like an ocean of greenery, occasionally broken by the protruding ruins of temples. He smelled the damp scents of approaching evening: night-blooming flowers from vines that curled through the leaves, the rich moistness of the Massassi trees themselves, a fine mist rising above the canopy as if the forest itself were exhaling in its sleep.

The looming coppery gas-giant of Yavin shimmered low in the sky like a dying ember, a huge sphere of swirling gases. Not far from the orangish planet, though invisible to Lowie's eye, orbited GemDiver Station, Lando Calrissian's mining operation that retrieved valuable Corusca gems from the gas-giant's core.

Lowie looked away from the planet setting on the horizon, though, as deeper night seeped into the sky. Specks of starlight dusted the midnight blue canopy.

Finding a comfortable spot to lean against the outspread crown of the Massassi tree, he remained still, breathing deeply, drawing comfort from the sight of the endless trees . . . and thinking of Kashyyyk.

He should be calm, but he was very worried about his sister. He could do nothing to help her, and she had to make her own choices—and face the consequences of those choices. Even so, Lowie understood the dangers she intended to face deep in the underlevels of the rain forest on the Wookiee planet.

He ran his long, strong fingers over the pearly strands of his fiber belt, woven from threads harvested from the deadly jaws of the carnivorous syren plant. It had been quite an ordeal for him to obtain those strands, but he had succeeded. Alone.

Lowie sat still as the air cooled and the noises of the jungle grew louder. Evening insects and predators stirred and went about their business.

At his side the miniaturized translating droid, Em Teedee, remained silent—switched off, so that Lowie could ponder his concerns without being interrupted by synthesized chatter. He sat back, and time passed. He would be late for evening meal back at the Jedi academy, but he didn't mind.

He had more important things to worry about.

By the time Jaina Solo finished her meal inside the Great Temple, most of the other Jedi trainees had left the eating area. Preoccupied, she slurped the last morsels of roasted crab nuts and salted boffa fruit, dabbing up the juice with a chunk of fresh bread.

Beside her at the table, her twin brother Jacen had only half finished his meal; a droplet of greenish syrup ran unnoticed down his chin. Jacen spoke excitedly, his brandy-brown eyes blinking as he ran a hand through his tousled brown hair.

"And I did manage to catch that stinger lizard down in the hangar bay. It's taken me weeks to coax him out of hiding. He's all by himself now in that new cage you built for me, but I'm not sure what he eats." He paused briefly to stuff some food into his mouth.

Jaina nodded, only half listening. She was

concerned that Lowbacca hadn't shown up to eat. Their Wookiee friend had been reserved lately, keeping to himself, speaking little even to his closest friends.

"Not to mention that several of the cocoons for my beetle moths are about to hatch!" Jacen continued. "I think I'm going to let most of them go, but I want to keep two as specimens, to see if they'll lay eggs in captivity. And you should see the fascinating blue fungus I found in a crack between some stones down by the river."

He gulped more juice, then suddenly held up a finger as he remembered something. "Oh yes, I've been meaning to ask—could you check the cage for my crystal snake? I think he's up to some mischief, maybe even trying to break out again—and you *know* what trouble that would cause."

Jaina couldn't help indulging in a quick giggle, remembering the pandemonium the nearly invisible snake had caused the last time it had gotten loose: the serpent had bitten the uppity student Raynar, sending the boy instantly to sleep. Not all of Jacen's pets caused trouble, though. Another crystal snake had helped to divert the lost TIE pilot Qorl from his attack on the Jedi academy, shortly after the twins had found Qorl living in self-imposed exile deep in the jungles of Yavin 4.

Jaina had hoped the old TIE pilot might have a soft spot for them after their efforts to help him, but Qorl had chosen not to become their ally. Instead, the Imperial brainwashing he had undergone resurfaced and became even more deeply entrenched. The pilot had returned to the remnants of the Empire, where he had fallen in with the Shadow Academy.

Jaina nodded to her brother, shaking herself from her reverie. "Okay, I'll take a look at the crystal snake cage."

She whirled as she heard the tinny mechanical voice of Em Teedee saying, "Master Lowbacca, I must urge you to ingest a wider variety of nourishment than that. According to your species' nutritional requirements, those foods are insufficient for a growing Wookiee to maintain a healthy level of energy . . . though I must admit you *have* been sulking lately instead of engaging in physical activities. Your diet should consist primarily of large quantities of fresh meat, which is substantially higher in protein than those fresh fruits and vegetables you're presently consuming."

Lowbacca answered with only a half-hearted growl as he carried his food into the eating area. Without even looking for his friends among the other Jedi trainees, he sat by himself at a small table against the stone wall.

"Lowie!" Jaina got up and hurried over to the ginger-furred Wookiee. "We were worried about you. You didn't come join us for the meal."

Lowie grunted something too brief for Em Teedee to translate.

Jaina pulled up a wooden chair across from their Wookiee friend and straddled it. Tucking a long strand of straight brown hair behind her right ear, she looked with concern at Lowie's shaggy head. The Wookiee turned his golden eyes down and studied the fruits and greens on his platter.

"Lowie, will you please tell us what's wrong?" Jaina said. "You can talk to us. We're *friends*, remember? Friends help each other."

Em Teedee spoke before Lowbacca could respond. "He won't answer you, Mistress Jaina. Even *I* can't get a response out of him. I'm afraid I'll never understand Wookiee behavior. Do all biological creatures have these unpredictable moods?"

Jacen sat down beside his sister. "Hey, maybe Lowie just wants to be left alone."

The young Wookiee groaned and nodded

dejectedly. Jaina sighed, gradually realizing that perhaps the best thing she could do for her friend would be to respect Lowie's wishes and let him solve his problems on his own. He knew he could talk to Jaina or Jacen anytime he wanted—but right now he didn't want to.

"All right," Jaina said, maintaining her deeply troubled expression, "but remember we're here for you, whenever you need us."

Lowie nodded, then stretched out one hairy arm to clasp Jaina's hand in his. The Wookiee's large grip engulfed her entire hand. During the brief touch, she reached out with the Force, hoping to find a clue to Lowie's strange behavior, but all she sensed was warmth and friendship.

Jaina stood up and gestured to her brother. "Come on, Jacen. Let's have a look at that crystal snake cage."

Lightsabers flared into the night, reflecting off the ancient stone walls of the Great Temple. Tenel Ka gripped the carved rancor-tooth handle of her new weapon as its brilliant turquoise beam pulsed through the activating crystal, a precious rainbow gem of Gallinore she had taken from her own royal tiara.

The warrior girl stood in the flagstoned

courtyard at the side of the ziggurat temple, a newly refurbished training area the students had reclaimed from the ever-encroaching jungle. The hardworking Jedi candidates had cleaned and polished the carefully set stones for exercises just such as this.

Tenel Ka gazed across at the alien mother-of-pearl eyes, elven features, and long quicksilver hair of her opponent—Tionne, the Jedi trainer and historian who often assisted Master Skywalker. The Jedi woman used her lightsaber with precision, matching Tenel Ka's moves stroke for stroke.

During an earlier training accident, Tenel Ka's poorly constructed lightsaber had exploded, and her friend Jacen's lightsaber blade had severed her left arm. Now Tenel Ka lived and fought with only one hand. But she wielded her glowing energy blade with strength and confidence.

Although skilled biotechnicians had offered her the best prosthetic arm replacement in the Hapes Cluster, Tenel Ka had turned them down. She prided herself in *being* herself—relying on her own abilities, her own strength and prowess. She did not want the artificial assistance of a biomechanical limb. Instead, she chose to alter her means of achieving her goal. She was determined to be as strong and as capable as ever before.

And when Tenel Ka determined to do something, she usually accomplished it.

Bright lights on the cleared landing grid in front of the temple illuminated the jungle, attracting thousands of nocturnal insects and the flying predators that fed on them. In the flagstoned courtyard, though, only the flares and flashes of intersecting lightsaber blades disturbed the night, bathing the area in a dazzling multicolored glow.

Tionne countered the warrior girl's stroke. "Very good, Tenel Ka," the teacher said. "You are learning to focus on precision rather than brute strength, to anticipate my moves and your own reactions using the Force."

Tenel Ka nodded, and her heavy red-gold braids danced around her head. The beads she had woven into the braids jingled and clacked together. She fought harder, sensing the control and skill of this older Jedi, who had been training for more than ten years now.

Several other students had come out to watch the exercises. All of Master Skywalker's Jedi candidates had intensified their training efforts, now that the New Republic was sure of the growing threat posed by the Shadow Academy and the Second Imperium. For more than a thousand generations, Jedi Knights had been the forces of light throughout the galaxy, and Luke Skywalker intended to continue the tradition.

Tionne swung her weapon with a calm, smooth gesture so unexpected that Tenel Ka barely reacted in time. She had sensed no intention of a counterattack from the silver-haired scholar, and so Tionne had surprised her. Their blades locked and sizzled—and then Tionne pulled her lightsaber back.

"Halt," she said, and switched off her weapon, leaving the warrior girl to stand with her own lightsaber blazing in her hand.

Tionne gestured up into the night sky of Yavin 4. The other students around the flagstoned courtyard stood up to watch. Just then, the twins Jacen and Jaina emerged from a low stone arch in the side of the Great Temple, hoping to observe Tenel Ka at her exercises. Instead, they all saw a glowing light streaking toward them like a tiny meteor.

"Hey, it's a ship!" Jacen said.

"Not just any ship," Jaina added. "I'd recognize it anywhere!"

Jacen blinked. "Hey, Dad never told us he was coming!"

Within a few moments the ship swooped down with a roar of its sublight engines and powered-up repulsorlifts. The flat, pronged disk of the *Millennium Falcon* settled with a loud hiss onto the landing pad.

Talking excitedly with each other, Jacen and Jaina rushed from the courtyard out onto the close-cropped weeds of the landing field to greet their father. The modified light freighter's boarding ramp extended, and Han Solo strode down it. A lopsided grin appeared as his children greeted him with wild enthusiasm.

When Chewbacca bounded down the ramp, Tenel Ka heard a bellow of greeting from behind her. She turned to see Lowbacca on one of the pyramid's stone ledges above the training area. He swung himself over the ledge and scrambled down the sloping temple blocks to reach the ground. Chewbacca roared a response to his nephew.

Lowbacca had been very troubled recently, and Tenel Ka could sense many deep thoughts working through his brain. She had decided to honor her Wookiee friend by letting him fight his own battles . . . unless he asked for help. But when she saw the expressions on

Chewbacca's and Lowie's faces, Tenel Ka grasped a strange and interesting fact.

Although the twins had been surprised by the unexpected appearance of the *Millennium Falcon*, Lowbacca had known full well that the ship was coming.

2

JAINA REALIZED SHE was grinning like an idiot as she hugged her father. "What are you doing here? We didn't even know you were coming."

Beside her, Jacen gaped at Han Solo's unfamiliar costume of tattered cloth and furs. His hair had been cut raggedly, and he looked much tougher. "Blaster bolts, Dad! Why are you dressed like that?"

Before Han Solo had a chance to reply, Jaina glanced behind him. Even in the dimness she could see that some of the *Millennium Falcon*'s plating had been replaced with dark anodized hunks of metal, new storage pods had been mounted on the bow, and a second transmitting dish was attached to the rear. Her jaw dropped. "And what did you do to the *Falcon*? It looks so . . . different!"

"One question at a time, kids," Han said, laughing and holding his hands palm out at chest level, as if to ward off an oncoming charge. "There've been a few problems in the Outer Rim recently, so in her official capacity, the New Republic's Chief of State—"

"You mean Mom," Jaina said.

"Right." Han's grin was boyish. "Anyway, she's been after me and Luke to do some scouting for her. Says I need to keep busy or I'll get old too fast. And ever since he started this Jedi academy, your uncle's made it a practice to spend some time away from Yavin 4, just to make sure his skills stay at their peak performance. Still, we figured it might be a good idea to keep a low profile, though, so—"

"You disguised yourself and the *Millennium Falcon*," Jacen finished for him. Jaina continued to stare at all the lumpy, patchwork modifications to the light freighter.

"And Luke, too." Han Solo nodded behind them to where their uncle, clad in a rumpled brown flight suit, emerged from the base of the temple. "Hey, Han, did you bring the last components for those new shield generators?" Luke called. He brushed a greasy hand down the front of his stained outfit. He looked very much like a down-and-out pilot who had deserted his post.

"You bet, Luke," Han said. "Leia's worried

about your Jedi academy with the Second Imperium on the loose, so we've got to install those new shield generators and get them running with enough power to stop an attack."

"I still think my Jedi Knights would do a good enough job defending themselves if it came to that," Luke said, smiling at the trainees standing around the temple. "The Shadow Academy would be foolish to underestimate us."

Han shrugged. "Doesn't matter what you say, Luke—indulge me, or Leia will never sleep a wink."

Laughing, Luke called for Jedi students to unload the heavy components from the *Falcon*'s storage bay. "I'll have some of my students install the systems while you and I are away."

The disguised Jedi Master strode over to the pair of Wookiees, who stood in earnest conversation. He seemed to be bidding Chewbacca farewell. Jaina thought she heard Luke say something about the time being near, but before she could ask about it, her brother spoke up.

"But what about Chewie?" Jacen asked. "Isn't he going to be your copilot this time?"

Their father looked a bit uncomfortable.

"I'll manage without him somehow. Back home on Kashyyyk, he and Lowie have kind of a family emergency, you might say."

"Emergency?" Jaina said. "Is anyone hurt?"

"Naw, nothing that simple. You've never met Lowie's sister Sirra, have you?" Han lifted his chin to point in the direction of his Wookiee copilot, who was deep in conversation with Lowbacca. "Anyway, give the two of 'em a chance to talk first. Afterwards I have a feeling Lowie'll tell you all about it. Meanwhile, I've brought messages from your mom and Anakin—and I've got a couple of surprises for you on the *Falcon*."

"Uh-oh," Jaina said. "*More* surprises on the *Falcon*?"

Han chuckled and put an arm around each of the twins' shoulders. "Yeah, presents for you two."

"Hey, that reminds me," Jacen said, "I've got a new joke. Wanna hear it?" Before either of them could talk him out of it, he forged ahead. "What do Jawas have that no other creature in the galaxy has? Give up?" He raised his eyebrows. "*Baby Jawas!*"

Even their father had difficulty feigning amusement. Jaina studied her brother in silence for a moment, then turned to Han, getting back to the subject at hand. "So, what were you saying about those gifts you brought us?"

"Well, I brought a mate for Jacen's stump lizard, along with some of those starflower blossoms they like to eat so much, and a refurbished micromotivator that still needs some tinkering. 'Course, you two'll have to fight over who gets which gift," he added, ruffling the twins' hair as they walked up the boarding ramp together.

Jaina snorted indelicately. "That shouldn't take long."

In her quarters, Tenel Ka sat fascinated by the tiny holographic image of dark-haired Anakin Skywalker holding a cluster of brightly colored twine. She couldn't figure out why the twins' little brother would have sent *her* a message. She had only met the boy once, on Coruscant not long ago.

"I know how independent you are, Tenel Ka, so I hope you don't mind my doing this," Anakin's recorded voice said. "But when Jacen and Jaina told me how hard it is for you to braid your hair since the accident, I took it as a problem to solve. You may have figured out a bunch of this stuff for yourself already"— Anakin's holographic face smiled faintly—

"but even if you have, it was still a challenging puzzle, and I enjoyed it."

The Solo twins, who had delivered the holographic message to Tenel Ka after a long visit with their father, sat nearby on the floor of her chambers. Jaina rolled her eyes and chuckled. "That's my little brother."

"This is a fact," Tenel Ka said, shifting her concentration back to the glowing hologram.

The boy's image held the multicolored twine in one hand and threaded the fingers of the other hand through it, neatly separating the colors into individual clumps. Tenel Ka unconsciously lifted her hand to her head and threaded her fingers through some unbraided strands of her red-gold hair.

Moving with deliberate precision, Anakin slid his hands down the brightly colored strands, twining them together with the fingers of one hand as he went. "See, it can be done, if you approach the task from a different perspective." The sequence cycled through again in slow motion while Anakin said, "I tried adding decorations several ways, but it worked best for me if I put the bead or feather in my mouth first. That way I didn't have to let go of the braid to pick it up."

"Ah." Tenel Ka nodded her approval of the

logic. "Aha." Experimentally, her fingers began to twine a few strands of hair, following the single-handed technique Anakin had concocted.

The hologram shifted to a different scene, Anakin standing beside a fall of long glossy brown hair, caught up in a dozen Dathomiran warrior braids decorated with feathers and beads. The view pulled back, and Anakin gestured to his handiwork, looking both pleased and a bit embarrassed. "As you can see, Mom let me practice on her." The tiny holographic image of Chief of State Leia Organa Solo turned with a warm smile and then spun in a graceful pirouette to give a better view of the braids.

As the holorecording ended, Tenel Ka nodded seriously, considering the new technique. With practice, she thought she could manage it herself.

A loud questioning growl sounded from the doorway of Tenel Ka's quarters. She looked up to see Lowbacca standing at the arched entrance.

"Enter, friend," Tenel Ka said, indicating a spot on the floor beside her. "Sit with us if you wish."

"Lowie, is everything all right?" Jaina asked with a look of concern.

The lanky ginger-furred Wookiee ambled over and sat between Tenel Ka and Jaina on the floor. For a long time none of the companions spoke. Then Lowbacca reached toward his belt and flicked a small switch on Em Teedee's back. "Ah, thank you, Master Lowbacca," Em Teedee said. "That was indeed a refreshing shutdown cycle, although considerably longer than I had anticipated. Oh, look—we have company."

Lowbacca interrupted the little droid with a rumble and a short bark. "Why, most assuredly, Master Lowbacca. I'd be delighted to provide a translation. That *is* my primary function, you know. I am fluent in over six forms of communication."

Preoccupied, Lowbacca didn't even scold the translating droid. Slowly, haltingly at first, the Wookiee began to speak, and Em Teedee translated. "Master Lowbacca knows that his recent . . . *distress* has been apparent to all of you, causing you no small measure of concern—a concern shared by myself, I might add."

Jaina put a hand on Lowbacca's shoulder. "Well, you did have us worried. We wanted you to be able to talk to us."

"We're your friends," Jacen added.

Tenel Ka merely nodded and waited for Lowbacca to continue.

He squared his shoulders and went on with his explanation. "In recent months a family matter has arisen that has caused Master Lowbacca no end of worry over his sister Sirrakuk's safety.

"As you may recall, young Wookiees occasionally take it upon themselves to perform a feat of great danger and difficulty, either alone or accompanied by friends. This gains them much respect, especially at a time when they are choosing their life path.

"Master Lowbacca decided to prove himself with such an act of bravery, since he knew that it would be difficult for many Wookiees to accept his decision to train at the Jedi academy rather than follow a more traditional calling. He was so proud of his intellectual skills that he chose to rely only on his wits; he descended to the deep forest levels on Kashyyyk without telling a single friend. Alone, he harvested these fibers from the dangerous syren plant. Though Master Lowbacca emerged unharmed with the trophy he had sought, he now admits that his solo expedition was foolhardy and ill-advised. And he fears that Sirrakuk is considerably more impulsive, more impetuous than he."

Here Lowbacca paused to finger the glossy fiber of his webbed belt. Its intricate braiding reminded Tenel Ka of Anakin's message to her, his technique of one-handed braiding.

Jaina gave Lowie a measuring look. "Ah, so now you're afraid that your sister might try to go it alone just because you did?"

Lowbacca looked down at the floor and gave a series of low rumbles and growls. Resting both elbows on his furry knees, he held his head in his hands as he spoke.

"I'm afraid the situation is rather more serious than that, and Lowbacca believes that the responsibility is largely his," Em Teedee said. "You see, since childhood Sirra's best friend was Raabakyysh—or Raaba, as Master Lowbacca's family referred to her—intelligent, strong-willed, beautiful, and adventurous. In fact, Master Lowbacca had always felt that . . . Well, go on," the little droid prompted. "You thought that *what*? You can't simply stop in the middle of a sentence."

Lowie gave a low groan and began to speak again. The dark streak of fur over his eyebrow fluffed up, slowing his agitation.

"Approximately one month ago, Raaba prepared to show her own skills in the face of danger, since she wanted to join a difficult and exclusive pilots' school, hoping one day to become the captain of her own ship. Sirra and Raaba had agreed to accompany one another—but the night before they had planned to go, Raaba impulsively decided to go alone.

"In secret, she descended to the lower jungles at night, leaving behind nothing but a brief message to explain to Sirra what she had done and why. According to her note, Raaba had hoped that by duplicating Lowbacca's feat of bravery she might impress him enough that he would someday consider her a worthy mate for a Jedi—when they were old enough. However . . ."

Lowbacca paused and heaved a deep sigh before continuing. "However—oh dear!—I'm afraid Raaba never returned from her ordeal," Em Teedee continued. "When her family searched for her they found only her bloodstained toolpack. Nothing more. Raaba was gone."

"Oh, Lowie." Jaina leaned her head against the Wookiee's shoulder.

Tenel Ka looked at her friend, sensing his pain. "Ah. This is why you feel responsible."

Lowie spoke again, this time in strangled tones. "Since Raaba's . . . loss, Sirra has become increasingly reckless, as if she hardly cares whether she lives or dies. Sirra has refused all offers from other friends to accompany her on her rite of passage, insisting that Raaba was the only one she trusted enough to take along. A while ago, in desperation, Master Lowbacca sent Sirra a message asking if she would accept *him* as a suitable substitute. Chewbacca has just brought word of her answer." Em Teedee paused for a moment. "Oh, thank goodness—she's accepted!"

"Hey, that's great," Jacen said in a relieved voice.

"Oh, indeed," Em Teedee chirped.

Lowbacca didn't respond immediately. He seemed to be intently studying a chip in the flagstoned floor.

"Something's still bothering you, Lowie," Jaina said.

Tenel Ka glanced down at the stump of her severed left arm, then gave Lowie an understanding look. "You fear to face your loss. The loss of Raaba."

"That's it, isn't it?" Jaina said. "It's going to hurt to go back to Kashyyyk, because your friend Raaba won't be there. And you feel responsible that she died trying to copy something you did."

After Lowie's response, Em Teedee said, "Master Lowbacca is also concerned that his grief over the loss of Raabakyysh will render him less capable of supporting his sister at this critical time. He realizes that it may not be feasible, but he was hoping to impose on one of you to accompany him to his homeworld."

Tenel Ka answered immediately. "You came when I needed you, after my accident. I can do no less, my friend." She reached out her hand to touch Lowbacca's.

"Hey, I'll come too," Jacen said, placing his hand over both of theirs. "We're stronger together. All of us."

Jaina placed her hand over the others. "I guess we all go then," she said. "Stronger together."

Lowbacca hung back, standing near the disguised *Millennium Falcon* while the Solo twins said goodbye to their father.

Han Solo gave his kids a lopsided grin. "Yeah, I kinda had a hunch that all of you were gonna volunteer to go with Lowbacca," he said. "As soon as Chewie told me the situation, I cleared it with your mom. Should be a good opportunity for you kids to brush up on Wookiee language comprehension, too."

Just then Luke Skywalker, wearing his tattered jumpsuit, emerged from the hangar bay with Chewbacca. Lowie could smell the grease stains and solvents on the old fabric. "Everything ready?" Master Skywalker asked.

"Ready as it'll ever be," Han Solo replied with another grin. "You and Chewie finished prepping the *Shadow Chaser*?"

Luke turned to Chewbacca, who had come up beside him, and said, "The *Chaser*'s a good ship; don't let anything happen to her." The big Wookiee shrugged and gave a bark of agreement.

Han Solo thumped Chewie on the back. "Take care of yourself. I'm trusting you with my kids, you know. Keep 'em all in one piece, okay? We'll see you in a couple of weeks." With that, Han gave the twins one last hug and went aboard the *Millennium Falcon*.

Before walking up the ramp, Master Skywalker looked around at the young Jedi Knights with calm confidence. "Don't forget that you're stronger together," he said. "May the Force be with you."

When the departing *Falcon* was just a speck in the distance, its bank of sublight engines glowing white, Lowbacca heaved a sigh and growled questioningly at Jaina.

She chuckled. "Right. What are we waiting for?"

3

THE SLEEK *SHADOW CHASER*, with its Imperial design and oily-looking quantum armor, glistened in the early-morning sun as Chewbacca piloted it slowly out of the sheltered hangar bay beneath the Great Temple.

Jacen stood next to his sister and Tenel Ka, watching the vessel move under silent power. Considering Lowie's recent distress, Jacen was glad his uncle Luke had let them take the *Shadow Chaser*—just the kind of fast, stealthy ship needed for an urgent mission. He was proud that Lowie wanted them along, that he and his sister and Tenel Ka could be of some help to their Wookiee friend.

Lowie stood at the far end of the clearing, motioning with his shaggy arms to direct Chewbacca's piloting. When the *Shadow Chaser* came to a halt, its entry ramp extended. Chewbacca stood at the top, gestur-

ing with his cinnamon-furred arms and bellowing.

"Master Chewbacca cordially requests that
we all come aboard," Em Teedee translated,
speaking in a wobbly voice as he bounced
with each running step Lowie took.

Jacen slung his satchel of belongings over
one shoulder. He turned to see if he could
offer any assistance to Tenel Ka, but when he
saw the determined look in the warrior girl's
gray eyes, he decided he'd be better off if he
didn't ask.

They climbed aboard the *Shadow Chaser*
and waved a brief goodbye to the other students and Tionne, who held up a hand in
farewell. Even before the ship was completely
sealed and ready to take off, Tionne had ush-
ered the trainees back to their studies. With
the threat of the Second Imperium loose in the
galaxy, the new Jedi Knights had no time to
relax.

With a smooth surge of acceleration, so
powerful yet gentle it seemed almost to glide
against gravity, the *Shadow Chaser* aimed its
nose upward and arrowed straight into the
mist-shrouded skies of the jungle moon.

En route to Kashyyyk, Jacen watched Lowie
and Chewbacca in the two front seats of the

narrow cockpit as the *Shadow Chaser* lurched into hyperspace. When the pair spoke rapidly in the Wookiee language, they sounded like two ferocious beasts challenging each other— but Jacen knew it was just a conversation, though he could make out only a few words. Em Teedee had been instructed not to bother translating, so that Lowie and Chewie could have some uninterrupted words in relative privacy.

While his sister tinkered with her multi-tool, disassembling a tiny mechanical gadget she had brought from her workshop on Yavin 4, Jacen took the opportunity to amuse Tenel Ka. He decided that, rather than telling jokes this time, he would explain to the gruff girl *why* certain things were funny, why she should be laughing at his punch lines—well, some of them, anyway. Jacen had begun to wonder if perhaps the girl simply didn't understand, and that was why she didn't laugh.

After all, it couldn't be that *every one* of his jokes was bad.

He explained how ridiculous answers to straightforward-sounding questions were supposed to be funny. He showed her how doing unexpected things with food or simple items of clothing might be considered amusing.

Tenel Ka watched him gravely, with full and unwavering attention. But she never cracked a smile.

With a sigh, Jacen told a few of his best jokes, then gave her some of his worst, trying to explain the difference by way of example. Tenel Ka didn't laugh at either.

In desperation, he considered going to the food-prep unit, ordering a pan of chilled Deneelian fizz-pudding, and then comically tripping so that the entire mess splatted in his face—but by this time, Jacen figured that even such a spectacular pratfall would have no effect on the young warrior woman.

Shaking his head in surrender, Jacen decided to leave Tenel Ka alone. He would occupy himself with something less discouraging for the time being. His spirits instantly perked up as he reached out with Jedi senses and detected something interesting in the back of the *Shadow Chaser* . . . the faint glow of a life-form, some creature out of place by the engine compartments. Jacen decided to go snoop. Nobody else was likely to be interested, anyway.

In the shielded rear compartment beyond the sleeping bunks and the food-prep area, Jacen heard the pulsing, pounding thump of engines as the *Shadow Chaser* sped along through hyperspace. He looked at the intricate control panels and access grids, the weapons batteries charged with spin-sealed Tibanna gas, and the shield generators that projected a canopy of protection around the sleek ship. But through all the din and the vibrating power of the engines, Jacen could still detect the faint emanations of some small creature, lost and frightened.

"Don't be scared," Jacen said, speaking with his voice and at the same time thinking the words through the Force. "I'm your friend. I can help you. Let me see you. It's okay."

He lowered his voice to a whisper as he bent down, looking in crannies between the control grids. He followed his senses. "I won't hurt you. I just want to see you. I know you're afraid. You can trust me." He touched his fingers lightly to one of the cool metal access panels, gently brushing the ion shield generators with his mind.

He sensed the creature hiding back there, trembling, guarding something. A little nest?

"It's just me," Jacen said. "Relax. I'll take care of you."

He popped the metal covering off the access panel to the ion shield generator. Inside, in a comfortable little pocket of colorful debris, cowered a furry eight-legged rodent, a mouselike creature with puffy frost-gray fur. It looked up at him with tiny black eyes that glittered in the dim light. It wiggled its damp nose. Judging by the pair of long teeth that protruded from the center of its snout, this rodent was a gnawer, not a flesh eater.

"Come here," Jacen said. "That's not a safe place for you to be." He reached in and calmly drew the rodent out. Its eight legs trembled and tickled against his palm like a plump furry spider, but a friendly and gentle one.

Jacen stroked its back, then bent to peer at the nest again. The rodent had chewed tiny strips of insulation from the power cables, yanked threads and wires and fabrics and plastics from the shield generator to create a soft pocket in which squirmed four smooth cylindrical grubs, the creature's young.

"Oh, what a nice nest you have," Jacen said soothingly. "But I don't think you were supposed to use those components. We need this ion shield generator, you know. It protects the whole ship."

He continued stroking the rodent and retrieved the nest carefully so as not to disturb the young. He held the nest in his hand and placed the mother back on top, snuggled against her little ones. "I'll keep you safe,"

Jacen said, "but we'll have to tell Jaina and Lowie about this, so they can make repairs."

Preoccupied with calming his new pet, Jacen returned to the forward compartments. He went to his sister who was still tinkering with an incomprehensible mechanical gadget. "Hey, Jaina? I've got some bad news."

She turned, holding up a small hydrospanner. "What?"

Before he could answer, though, the *Shadow Chaser* gave a sudden lurch and rocked as if it had slammed into something invisible. The deck tilted sideways, throwing Jacen to his knees. He struggled to protect his new pet.

The colors of hyperspace swirled like a psychedelic flood in all directions out the windowports. When the *Shadow Chaser* gave another violent lurch, Jacen tumbled backward to the deck; it took all his concentration to guard the precious nest.

"Uh, never mind," he said. "It can wait."

Jaina gripped the armrests of her seat while the ship rocked back and forth. Her tools and the electronic di-scanner remote she had just repaired flew like projectiles to the bulkheads, then smashed onto the deckplates, ruined.

When the ship momentarily stabilized, her

brother crawled to his feet, cradling something in one arm, his hair even more tousled than usual. He checked to make sure Tenel Ka was okay. The warrior girl stood up, planting her booted feet wide apart, seeking balance as the *Shadow Chaser* shuddered and bucked its way through the disturbance.

"What is happening?" Tenel Ka said.

Ahead in the cockpit, Lowie and Chewbacca roared to each other, fighting the controls.

"An ion storm?" Em Teedee chimed in with an electronic wail. "Are you absolutely certain? We're doomed!"

Jaina's lips pressed into a tight, grim line. "It's an ion storm, all right. Just bad luck. Couldn't predict this. We plotted the shortest path to Kashyyyk using the navicomputer. The on-line catalogs only display stable astronomical hazards—star clusters, black holes, and high-energy nebulas—but ion storms come and go. They don't have any set position, but they sure ripple up hyperspace when you pass through 'em."

"Is it serious?" Jacen asked. Droplets of sweat broke out on his brow. "I've got a bad feeling about this."

"Just have to wait and see," Jaina said.

Tenel Ka stood with her hand to her utility

belt, ready to fight some tangible foe with a throwing knife, her lightsaber, even her fibercord. But none of those would do any good against an ion storm.

Chewbacca and Lowie grappled with the controls, hairy fingers flying over panels, yanking levers. The *Shadow Chaser* winked out of hyperspace and lurched back into the fringes of the furious ion storm.

"Uh-oh," Jacen said. "I forgot to tell you that we might have some damage to our ion shield generator." He held up the nested bundle of wires and insulation.

Jaina whirled, more worried than ever. "Oh, no! That could—"

As the *Shadow Chaser* plummeted into the space storm, they were immediately surrounded by a spiderweb of high-energy lightning bolts, powerful discharges that arched across the seething knot of hot gas that formed the unexpected interstellar hurricane. The ship thrashed like a mad bantha, throwing its passengers about.

Jacen braced his shoulder against a control bar, and Tenel Ka fell into him. He held the warrior girl upright, pinning both of them against the wall, still cradling his newfound pet in one hand. Jaina, trying to struggle toward the cockpit, fell flat on her face.

The *Shadow Chaser*'s rear engines kicked in, and the sublight drive heaved them away from the rippling ion cloud. In the pilot seat Chewbacca groaned, gripping the controls and wrestling to keep them on a straight course, the shortest path out of danger.

Lowie cried out as fingernails of icy blue electricity skittered across the control panels, burning out subsystem after subsystem.

Behind the back bulkheads, the straining ion shield generators squealed loudly in surrender. Then, with a loud bang, they fell silent.

The rippling colors dwindled outside the cockpit window, and the *Shadow Chaser* careened onward, spiraling out into open space, safe at last from the storm. Still, Jaina shuddered to think of how much damage the stray ion bursts must have caused.

Jacen brushed himself off and forced a lopsided grin. "Now, uh, as I was saying about that damage to the ion shields . . ." He held out the eight-legged rodent, which cowered in her nest, as if she comprehended the trouble she had caused. "I found this critter's nest in the machinery. I took her out, but I needed one of you to fix the damage."

"It would appear that we now have plenty

of time to fix it," Tenel Ka said. "We are *capable* of fixing it, are we not?"

From the cockpit Lowie and Chewie consulted in growling voices.

"Oh, excellent!" Em Teedee said. "Master Lowbacca says we have been quite lucky. Our propulsion and life-support systems are largely intact and can be repaired quite easily. My, that *is* wonderful news."

Em Teedee fell silent as the Wookiees continued, and then the little droid piped up. "Excuse me—what did you say, Master Lowbacca? Oh dear! It seems, however, that our navicomputer has been completely disabled. We have lost all coordinates for getting from here to anywhere else. Oh my. We're . . . we're lost in space."

Chewbacca and Lowie both roared in outrage at the translating droid, and Em Teedee quickly fell silent. "Well, I suppose I *should* find it comforting that you both have such confidence in your navigational abilities," Em Teedee muttered after a moment.

The two Wookiees busily consulted with each other and began punching and programming numerical values into the navigational control panel, double-checking each other's calculations. Before long, after everyone had helped with temporary repairs, the *Shadow Chaser* was on its way again.

At first Jaina was surprised that they were back on course—then she realized that she shouldn't have been. After all, Kashyyyk was the only Wookiee planet, and both Lowie and Chewbacca greatly revered the place.

Why should she find it unusual that they had both memorized the coordinates for their homeworld?

4

IN A SECLUDED meeting chamber at the
Shadow Academy, Zekk stood proudly, struggling to hide any sign of nervousness. He
raised his chin and waited to receive his
long-anticipated reward. It had come to this,
at last.

The air smelled cold and metallic, exhila-
rating. Brilliant light stabbed down from the
metal ceiling, making him squint his emerald
eyes; the irises were ringed with a darker
corona, like the shadowy outline around his
personality. Zekk tossed back his shaggy dark
hair, one shade lighter than black, and looked
up, blinking, as Lord Brakiss approached him
in the harsh light.

The master of the Shadow Academy was
wrapped in rippling silvery robes of a fabric
that looked as if it might have been spun by
deadly spiders. Against one wall, wearing her
spined and glittering black cloak, stood
Tamith Kai, the fierce commander of the new

Nightsisters. Her violet eyes burned beneath a generous mane of ebony hair.

Beside Tamith Kai waited two other prominent Nightsisters—attractive and petite Garowyn and muscular Vonnda Ra, both from the planet Dathomir. In their black-spined capes and lizard-hide armor, the three Nightsisters reminded Zekk of hungry birds of prey.

Next to them, the grizzled TIE pilot, Qorl, stood at attention, surrounded by a stormtrooper escort of his most promising Imperial trainees. Beneath the white armor, one of the burliest of these was the gangleader Norys, who had led the Lost Ones on Coruscant not long ago. While the other stormtroopers stood rigidly at attention, weapons shouldered, Norys fidgeted and seemed angry and uncomfortable with the ceremony. His senses finely tuned by his own anxiety, Zekk could pick up the harsh muttering words from behind the bully's white helmet. "Trash collector . . . gets all the breaks."

Moving quietly and unobtrusively, Qorl rested his powerful droid replacement hand on the stormtrooper's shoulder armor in a gesture that was firm and clearly meant to quiet the bully. Zekk knew Qorl's droid arm was powerful enough to crack the white armor like an eggshell. Norys fell silent, though he obviously remained upset.

Zekk didn't mind. This was his moment of glory, and he smiled faintly at the thought of how much had changed in only a few months—and how now he had arrived at the peak of his triumph.

For this presentation and initiation, Zekk had worn his new leather uniform; heavy round studs decorated the reinforced pads on his shoulders, creating a kind of armored hide. His hands were encased in thick black gloves that made a warm, satisfying creak as he clenched and unclenched his fists.

Brakiss's porcelain-perfect face smiled with pride. He held out a gift, a flowing black cape lined with deep, vibrant crimson, like fresh dark blood.

"Young Zekk, I present this to you as a symbol of your importance to the Shadow Academy," Brakiss said. "You have proven to be an avid pupil, a true asset to the Second Imperium. Our efforts would be greatly disadvantaged had you not joined us in our struggle. In your duel to the death with Vilas, our other powerful candidate, you proved yourself to be our champion, our new hope—our Darkest Knight."

Zekk blinked back stinging tears of pride and accomplishment as Brakiss draped the heavy fabric over his padded shoulders, then fastened the cape at his throat with a clasp shaped like a ferocious silver scarab.

Zekk watched Tamith Kai, who stood coiled with deadly energy, like a rogue assassin droid. He saw the tall Nightsister flinch at the mention of the slain Vilas, who had been her student, her candidate for the Shadow Academy's champion. But Zekk had defeated the surly, overconfident young man, and now *he* wore the black cape . . . while Vilas was little more than space dust ejected from the garbage port.

Brakiss stepped back and folded his hands in front of him; silvery sleeves flowed down his wrists, swallowing up his manicured hands. "The time has come for you to embark on your first important mission for us, Zekk. You will be given command of troops to prove your skills."

Zekk's heart leaped. He didn't think he could stand any more exhilaration in one day. "What," he stammered, "what do you wish me to do?"

"As a final stage in preparing for our attack on Rebel fortifications, we must launch another raid to obtain vital supplies. You will lead an assault team to the Wookiee world of Kashyyyk. There, in one of their technological tree cities, is the fabrication facility for the most sophisticated computer equipment used by our enemy's ships.

"If your raid is successful in obtaining guidance and tactical systems, we will have an enormous advantage in our overall conflict. We will then be able to throw the Rebel fleet into confusion and use their own computers against them to transmit conflicting signals. We can also use these systems to mimic their secret ship ID patterns, so that Second Imperium fighters can travel freely in enemy territory by identifying themselves as Rebel ships.

"Because of the importance of this mission, you will be assigned a powerful team. I am giving you use of the new holographic disguises we have developed for just such an infiltration effort. Everything depends on you, Zekk. Do you feel up to the task?"

Zekk nodded enthusiastically. "Yes! Yes, I can do that for you."

Tamith Kai strode forward into the pool of bright light that poured down on Zekk. He turned to look at the tall, ominous woman. Her wine-dark lips curved down in a serious expression. As if pronouncing his doom, she said, "There is one other part of the plan. Through an intercepted transmission, we have learned that those troublesome young Jedi brats are even now on their way to Kashyyyk. They sent a message to say goodbye to their mother—luckily Qorl has been monitoring all comm traffic from the vicinity of Yavin 4 back to the capital world." She stared at her claw-like fingernails, as if she found something interesting there.

"We had originally planned to wait a few more weeks before conducting this raid, but now . . . the timing couldn't be more perfect." Her violet eyes flashed with pleasure. "Your second assignment is to make sure that Jacen and Jaina and their difficult friends are . . . removed, so that we can proceed with our galactic conquest without worrying about their meddling."

Zekk swallowed hard when he heard the new orders, but did not reply. Jacen, and especially his sister Jaina, had been good friends for much of his youth. They had parted ways, though, when the twins went off to the Jedi academy, abandoning Zekk to his squalid life in the underworld of Coruscant. He had had no hope for a bright future until the Shadow Academy found him.

"All right," Zekk said in a voice low and

hoarse. He tried to speak louder, not willing to let self-doubt show through. He had made his own choices, and now he had to follow through on them despite the difficulties his conscience might encounter. "All right," he repeated. "When do we leave?"

"As soon as possible," Tamith Kai answered.

In the outer docking bay of the Shadow Academy, Tamith Kai and the other two Nightsisters loaded the ship for its assault mission. The vessel, marked with neutral insignia, was a small cargo freighter stolen from a lost trader who had ventured too close to the Core Systems. Tamith Kai wondered idly if the trader still languished deep in an Imperial prison . . . or if the guards had gotten around to executing him yet, since the Second Imperium could never afford to let the man loose with his knowledge of the Core Systems and the commandeered freighter.

In the observation bubble above the docking bay, Qorl stood by the cloaking shield controls, monitoring preparations for the launch of the mission. The old pilot would not accompany them himself, but he had chosen a handful of the Second Imperium's newly constructed TIE fighters and bombers to be loaded into the freighter's cargo bay.

"We'll see if Brakiss was wrong to place confidence in his young pet," Tamith Kai murmured in her low, rich voice. "I still don't trust him. What is it Norys calls the boy— trash collector? I sense that Zekk hasn't yet given himself entirely over to the dark side."

Vonnda Ra frowned, her squarish face puzzled. "But after all the work he's done— look at his training. How can you question Zekk's abilities?"

"It is his *motives* I question, not his abilities. I had no such doubts about the loyalty of my Vilas."

Garowyn interrupted. "Perhaps, Tamith Kai. But Vilas is dead. Zekk proved to be a better fighter. Perhaps you're simply being a sore loser."

Tamith Kai's eyes flared like twin violet stars about to explode. "I am *not* a sore loser," she snarled.

"Obviously not," Garowyn said, turning away with an ironic smile.

Tamith Kai clenched her fists in rage. "I think Zekk still has feelings for those obnoxious Jedi twins. His friendship is not so easily given up." She calmed herself. Her lips, dark as overripe fruit, twisted into a smile. "That's why I made sure this mission would be more than just a simple raid. Let us watch how Zekk takes care of his other assignment."

Vonnda Ra stored a crate of weapons inside the cargo shuttle and went to fetch the heavy belts that carried their holographic-disguise generators. "I thought the computer guidance and tactical systems were our most important objective."

"For you, perhaps, and for the Second Imperium," Tamith Kai said, nodding distractedly, "but not for me."

Garowyn crossed her wiry arms over her small chest. "You may be my nominal superior, Tamith Kai, but I can set my own priorities as well. I'll assist you in this raid, but the main reason *I'm* going along is to retrieve our . . . stolen property."

"What stolen property?" Vonnda Ra asked, the belts and holographic control packs still dangling from her outstretched arms.

"Our greatest ship, our most ambitious design, with quantum armor and powerful weapons—the *Shadow Chaser*. It is the peak of the Second Imperium's engineering success, my one joy. But Skywalker and that traitorous girl from Dathomir tricked me into an escape pod and stole my own ship out from under me! The Jedi academy has been using it ever since. I had all but given up hope of ever regaining what was rightfully mine, but now I've learned that the Wookiee and the Jedi brats have taken my ship to Kashyyyk. Now is our perfect chance to retrieve what is ours."

"Well, if you do get the *Shadow Chaser*, there will be more room for us when we return in the assault shuttle, then," Vonnda Ra said.

Tamith Kai directed a cool stare at the short, bronze-haired Nightsister. At last she smiled, with just a trace of warmth. "So. I see we each have our own agendas," she said. "Let us hope we all succeed."

5

"WHY, CERTAINLY, MASTER Lowbacca. I'd be happy to be of service in such a manner," Em Teedee said as they approached Kashyyyk. "Calculation of that trajectory is really quite simple."

Lowie accepted the finding from the little droid and input it manually on the *Shadow Chaser*'s control panel. Beside him, his uncle drew in a deep, happy breath when the rich brown-green planet appeared in the viewport, as if anticipating the tastes and smells and sounds of home. Despite the heavy heart with which he was returning, Lowie also felt a rush of excitement and pleasure. He would soon be in the safe, peaceful treetops of Kashyyyk.

"Well done, Masters Lowbacca and Chewbacca!" Em Teedee caroled. Lowie grunted an absentminded acknowledgment, still captivated by the sight of his planet. It looked much the same as it had on the day he left with his uncle and Han Solo in the *Millennium Falcon* to become a Jedi student. How long ago was it now?

Too long. Lowie's yearning to see his family again became almost overwhelming. The two Wookiees worked at the piloting controls with an urgency that came from happy anticipation. As the *Shadow Chaser* approached the thick canopy below, Chewbacca pointed with a certain wistfulness toward the treetop city in which he and Lowie's mother had grown up. With all of Chewie's travels across the galaxy, Lowbacca wondered if his uncle ever felt as homesick as he himself occasionally did on Yavin 4. He knew Chewbacca would somehow find the time to visit his own city and the rest of his family in the next day or so.

Behind him, the twins and Tenel Ka uttered exclamations of admiration at the beauty of Kashyyyk and the size of the trees. "Even though I've been here before, I always forget how big they are," Jaina murmured, pressing her fingers against the windowport.

"Impressive," Tenel Ka agreed. "But where are the cities?" Chewbacca let the sleek ship dip a bit lower, and Lowie pointed to where clusters of high trees extended their crowns above the lower canopies. Nestled in the masses of thick branches, gleaming towers and platforms were visible, signs of habitation that folded into the natural formation of the trees. "Ah," she said, sounding somewhat surprised. "Aha."

"Neat, huh?" Jacen said, leaning closer to the warrior girl. "They like to make nature and technology work together."

Lowie growled his agreement. "Master Lowbacca points out that technology and nature need not be mutually exclusive," Em Teedee translated. "Blending the two can be more pleasant than separating them."

When he finally caught sight of his home city, Lowie felt a renewed impatience. It was all he could do to keep himself from unbuckling his crash webbing while Chewbacca guided their damaged ship toward the nearest landing platform.

The moment the *Shadow Chaser* touched down, Lowbacca sprang from the copilot's seat and rushed to the exit hatch. Through the cockpit window, he could see his family waiting for him on the platform—his father, Mahraccor; his mother, Kallabow; and his younger sister, Sirrakuk.

Lowie opened the hatch and stood in the sunlight for a split second, taking in every detail, sniffing the air, letting his eyes be bombarded by the rich greens and browns of the treetops. Then he and his family all roared greetings. His parents looked well and happy, if a little tired. His mother's kind blue eyes, surrounded by auburn whorls of fur, shone with pride. The dark streak in his father's fur showed no signs of graying with age.

Only his sister looked different—taller, sleeker and prettier than he had remembered her, but with a heavy sadness about her face. Sirra had trimmed her fur in unusual patterns, had shaved decorative designs around her head and arms. But her fangs were white and sharp, the fur around her nose and mouth well-groomed and long. She was definitely growing up.

His father raised both arms over his head and bellowed another greeting. Lowie roared back and ran toward them.

Jacen looked around the dining table in consternation, wishing for the tenth time that he understood the Wookiee language better. Ensconced between Lowie and Sirra, he looked across the table to where Jaina and Tenel Ka sat on either side of Chewbacca; he wondered if they felt as confused and overwhelmed as he did in the middle of the loud and incomprehensible dinner conversation.

Transparent mesh cages filled with swarms of tiny, luminescent bugs hung from the ceiling branches, providing a fuzzy, warm light. Exotic spices and incense wafted around the room and out the open window notches into the humid night. The air was thick with mouthwatering smells of the welcome meal Lowie's parents had prepared.

The table was a huge slab of wood, a slice from a broad-boled tree: its hypnotic concentric rings indicated how long the tree had lived. All the chairs and furniture in Lowie's home seemed overlarge, built for bodies much taller than the average human. Jacen shifted uncomfortably on the high bench at the table.

Something finally clicked in his head. "Hey, where's Em Teedee?" he asked. "We could really use his translating skills here."

Jaina flushed, her mouth forming a small "oh" of surprise. "I, um, guess that's my fault," she stammered. "I kind of borrowed him and hooked him up to the *Shadow Chaser*'s diagnostics so he could give us a readout of the parts we need to repair the ship." She bit her lower lip. "I suppose it would have been more polite to wait until *after* we had

had a chance to chat with Lowie's family a while."

Jacen shrugged and squeezed his eyes shut. He tried to concentrate in the new environment, to pick out individual words. But with five Wookiees barking, bellowing, growling, and roaring, it was difficult to make sense of their speech. He took a slow breath and tried to relax, planning to reach out with the Force to see if he could sense some meaning in the conversation.

Outside, Jacen could hear a warm afternoon rain running gentle fingers through the leaves of the stately wroshyr trees. Inside, the battle of tones continued, strange voices mixing with familiar ones. In the undertones, he felt joy and apprehension, hope and sorrow. He felt . . .

He felt the touch of a furry hand on his arm. Jacen looked up in embarrassment to find Lowie's sister Sirra holding out a platter laden with roasted meats and vegetables. Sirra uttered a polite but curious woof.

"Blaster bolts! I'm sorry, is that plate for me?"

Lowie chuffed a laugh and then swept a hand around the table to indicate that everyone else had already been served. Each of the Wookiees' plates was filled with coarsely chopped fresh meat and mounds of raw vegetables. Jaina had a platter of food similar to his own, while Tenel Ka's held a mixture of vegetables and meats, both cooked and raw. Jacen was amused to note that Tenel Ka's appetite reflected the conflicting preferences of her primitive and refined upbringings. Kallabow and Mahraccor had worked hard to accommodate the dietary preferences of their human guests. Jacen accepted the platter from Sirra and thanked her.

When the Wookiees all fell silent, expectant, and turned to Lowbacca, he held one furry hand over his plate of food as he crooned a few short phrases in a low voice. Jacen recognized the Wookiee ceremonial speech of thankfulness that he had heard from Chewbacca so often.

Lowie stood then, raised his arms high and spread his hands as if forming a protective leafy canopy over his family and friends, and repeated his brief speech. Lowie's mother crooned a sad, low note.

A moment later, both Wookiees and humans attacked their food as if none of them had had a decent meal for weeks.

The next day, Jaina murmured something noncommittal and looked dubiously at the list that Em Teedee had downloaded to her datapad. Jacen and Tenel Ka sat near her in Lowie's spacious room, which had been hollowed out from part of a massive wroshyr tree. Lowie disconnected the lead wires from the diagnostics panel, tucked them back into Em Teedee's casing, and closed it with a snap. While Jaina and Lowie worked together to catalog the *Shadow Chaser*'s ills, Chewbacca had taken the opportunity to go to the other side of the planet to visit the rest of his family, whom he had not seen in some time.

A few leftover spatters of rain from another brief shower dripped outside the open window. Sirra sat with them, her patchy fur standing on end. She didn't want to be alone, apparently, but she didn't participate much in the conversation either.

"Take a look at this, Lowie," Jaina said, holding up the datapad.

The Wookiee studied the list of ruined components with a thoughtful growl. Jacen and Tenel Ka crowded in to get a look as well. Jacen flashed his sister a mischievous grin. "Hard to believe that an itty-bitty ion storm could cause so much damage, huh?"

Jaina sent him a withering look. "If that furry pet of yours hadn't chewed all the circuits—"

"Hey, that's not fair! I'd never even seen her before we left Yavin 4." Jacen removed the fluffy creature from the temporary cage he had made for her and her babies. The little eight-legged rodent seemed very pleased with her soft new nest. "She didn't mean to cause any trouble—did you, Ion?"

He held the fluffy ball close to his face and stroked her with one finger. The tiny creature made a faint cooing sound. Jacen would set the rodent free when they returned to Yavin 4, but for now he would take good care of her.

"The fault was not Jacen's," Tenel Ka said in a mild voice. "And blaming the creature serves no purpose."

Jaina shrugged one shoulder. "Yeah, I know. I'm sorry. Just don't let Chewie catch sight of that pesky little thing when he gets back tonight."

Lowie handed the datapad back to Jaina with a confident bark. "Master Lowbacca believes that we can obtain most of these parts at the local fabrication facility, or create reasonable substitutes," Em Teedee said.

Jaina felt hopeful. "You mean the factory where your parents work?"

"Blaster bolts," Jacen said. "Are you sure? There's a lot of stuff on that list. What do they make at the factory, anyway?"

Lowie gestured with his hands and growled an answer. Jaina could vaguely sense what he was saying. Em Teedee said, "The fabrication facility that employs Master Lowbacca's parents, as well as most of the other inhabitants of this tree city, produces a variety of sophisticated computer equipment for use in a wide range of transportation applications."

Jaina's interest sharpened at the idea of a factory filled with exotic and complex systems.

"Like what?" Jacen asked, placing Ion back in her cage. The little rodent inspected her grubs, rooting around in her fuzzy nest.

After more of Lowie's growling and gesticulating, Em Teedee said, "Among other things, the facility produces guidance control systems for planetary control towers, navigational subsystems and backups, tactical systems, communication encryption generators, multiphasic—"

"Hey, I think we get the idea. Thanks, Em Teedee," Jacen broke in.

Jaina tried to suppress a chuckle. Her ever-curious brother had gotten more explanation than he had bargained for. "Lowie, is there any way we can move the *Shadow Chaser* closer to your home so we can work on it more easily? The hangar bay where we stored it is way on the other side of the city. Not very convenient, if you know what I mean."

Lowie shook his head, but growled a suggestion. "Master Lowbacca proposes—" Em Teedee began.

"Yeah, I think I got it," Jaina said, struggling to understand a few of the Wookiee words. "We can pull out the damaged subsystems one or two at a time, bring them here to Lowie's house, and work on 'em." She beamed. "That's a great idea. So what are we waiting for?"

6

THE MORNING BREEZE ruffled Lowie's ginger-colored fur as he stood with his friends outside on the treetop observation platform. The area was broad and smooth, empty of equipment or visitors—the perfect place for them to stretch their muscles and perform Jedi exercises in the fresh outdoors.

The air was enriched with the scent of spring blossoms, new leaves, and sun-warmed wood. Beside him on the wooden platform, Sirra crouched in pensive silence, watching the Jedi trainees as they worked through their individual exercise routines.

Lowie tried not to make it obvious that he was keeping an eye on Sirra. Too great a show of concern on his part, he figured, would probably only annoy his sister and make her more stubborn. They had left many issues unspoken between them, but he knew they would have to talk soon.

He flicked his golden eyes around the platform and watched as Jacen did push-ups and Jaina practiced gymnastic tumbles. Tenel Ka, limber as ever, stood on one leg, the other pulled up high behind her, pointing toward the sky.

Lowie bent over, placed both hands flat on the warm wood of the platform, kicked his feet into the air, and balanced there. When Jaina turned a cartwheel past him, he risked another look at Sirra. His brash younger sister had spoken very little since his arrival yesterday, though she had instinctively remained close to him. Lowie couldn't help wondering what she was thinking. Did Sirra in any way resent him because he had inherited Jedi potential, while she had not? Did she blame him for Raaba's death? Did she resent the friends he had brought home with him?

He and his sister were so different that Lowie wondered if there had ever been a time when they understood each other completely. Lowie was thoughtful, analytical, introspective, while Sirra was wild, confident, outspoken. He preferred not to draw attention to himself, while she enjoyed surprising people with her appearance—why else would she trim the fur at her ankles, knees, wrists, and elsewhere in such a strange patchwork style?

Sirra and Lowie had always trusted one another, though—but did she *still* trust him?

Tenel Ka whirled through Lowie's field of vision, performing aerial somersaults. He felt himself begin to lose his balance, but quickly regained it and began doing vertical push-ups.

"Hey, Lowie," Jacen yelled from behind him, "can you spare a little concentration from your exercises to teach us a few words in your Wookiee dialect?"

Lowie grunted his assent. "Master Low-bacca says he would not be averse to the possibility of instructing you," Em Teedee translated.

Jaina chuckled. "Gee, that's funny, Em Teedee—it sounded to me like all he said was 'yes.'"

"Well, I suppose that *is* an alternate trans-lation," Em Teedee said, sounding somewhat miffed. "Though it's rather unimaginative."

Lowie gave a bark of laughter and looked over at Sirra to see if she had listened to the interchange. She returned his look for a moment, then deliberately turned and sat with her back to him at the edge of the platform, dangling her legs over the side, above the leafy canopy far below. She stared down toward the unseen depths . . . where Raaba had disappeared.

"Well then," Em Teedee said, sounding hurt now, "once you've taught the others your dialect, Master Lowbacca, I suppose you won't require my services anymore."

"Of course we'll still need you, Em Teedee," Jaina said. "We'll never be able to understand *every* word Lowie says."

Lowie absently grunted his agreement, still looking at Sirra's hunched shoulders. It occurred to him that although he had come home to support her in this difficult time, he had no idea *how* to do it. Clearly, his presence alone was not enough. He wanted to try talking with her, but what if she had problems he couldn't solve? What if *he* was part of the problem, having set a dangerous example that his sister felt obligated to follow, though it might mean her death?

Still balanced on his hands but deep in thought about Sirra, Lowie lost his concentration and his balance again, this time with embarrassing results. He teetered precariously for a moment, trying to regain his equilibrium. Em Teedee let out a squeal of surprise, then Lowie toppled over, landing on his rear end with a loud thump.

Jaina rushed over, adding to the Wookiee's embarrassment. "Are you all right?"

Lowie wished his friends had ignored the entire incident. To Jaina's credit, as soon as she had determined he was unhurt, she made a hasty retreat and became absorbed in her exercises again, studiously pretending not to notice while Lowie picked himself up off the platform's floorboards and dusted off his fur.

Still a bit self-conscious at his clumsiness, Lowie told Em Teedee to shut down for a rest cycle as he ambled over and seated himself by Sirra at the platform's edge, letting his legs swing free beside hers. He waited for a while, hoping his withdrawn sister would say something, since he had no idea where to begin. Watching her out of the corner of his eye, he pondered again what had caused them to turn out so different from each other, how two such opposites could spring from the same set of parents.

Lowie had a strong aptitude for the Force, whereas Sirra showed neither potential nor interest in the Jedi Knights. Lowie's quiet introspective nature had always been a sharp contrast to her confident outspokenness— until recently, that is, when she'd become so quiet. And, while Lowie could sit engrossed for hours in the intricacies of a computer system, Sirra became restless quickly and longed for excitement and adventure. In addition, Lowie had always prided himself in being obedient, finding it simpler to do what was expected of him than to expend effort on meaningless acts of rebellion against authority.

At that thought, Lowie's eyes were drawn to the bands of close-cropped fur on Sirra's body. It was not a style sported by any adults that Lowie knew, and very few youth. He finally decided to ask her about it, hoping to start a conversation somehow. Lowie blurted out the question, asking if the style kept her cooler during warm weather.

Sirra shrugged. That was not why she did it.

A symbol of mourning, then? For Raaba?

Sirra snorted at the suggestion.

Rebellion, then?

Sirra thought for a moment before sighing in confusion, obviously at a loss about how to explain. She thought of it as . . . a way of showing on the outside what did not show on the *inside*: that she was different.

Lowie considered this, rumbling deep in his throat. He had thought it was already clear enough that everyone was different.

Sirra shook her head and sprang to her feet on the platform. Lowie saw at once that she was irritated, that he had misunderstood her, for his sister walked all the way around the edge of the platform before motioning for him to join her. When he did, he practically had to run to keep pace with her.

At last Sirra spoke again, her agitation apparent in her voice. She pointed to her shaved wrists and elbows, explaining in more detail that she did this to show others that she was not like *them*.

Lowie cocked his head quizzically, trying to think of a response, but Sirra resumed her explanation. She said that since she didn't have Force potential as he did, their parents had always just assumed that she would work in the fabrication facility. But Sirra had no wish to work there like everyone else did. She didn't enjoy assembling computers, and was only a mediocre programmer. She raised a fist and barked loudly—she wanted something much more exciting!

Lowie shook his head sternly. Wookiees could excel in engineering, in science, in piloting—anything they wanted to. But such success did not come easily. He nodded toward his friends to indicate how hard they were training at the moment. Lowie and Sirra walked together for a while in silence.

Jacen, Jaina, and Tenel Ka finished their

exercises and perched at the edge of the platform, looking down at the beautiful tree canopy. Jacen pointed. "Hey, Lowie—how do you say the name for those trees?"

Lowie barked the answer—wroshyr.

After he and Sirra had skirted the trio, Lowie asked his sister what she wanted to do with her life. Sirra groaned and shrugged uncertainly.

Lowie thought for a moment. Well, what did she *like* to do? he asked.

Sirra heaved a heavy sigh, spreading her hairy arms wide to encompass the forest and the sky. She loved to be out and around, to visit new places and learn new things. She enjoyed feeling free, the way Lowie himself did when he'd travel alone in his skyhopper. And Sirra liked making her own decisions, not being told what she had to do and when.

Lowie growled the names of distant cities of Kashyyyk, suggesting other factories, other jobs. Sirra waved a hand as if to brush the idea away. She wanted to do something important, something unusual. Her voice suddenly sounded resentful of Lowie and his Jedi friends. They had been given a tremendous opportunity, and she wanted one for herself.

The twins and Tenel Ka took turns reaching out with the Force to make temporary furrows in the leafy canopy below, as if a giant invisible bird of prey were skimming over the leaves in search of its quarry. Sirra grumbled in disgust and pointed to the Jedi trainees "racing" their Force furrows through the leaves, crisscrossing and intertwining them.

She would never squander talent like that, she insisted. Knowing that she soon intended to prove her strength and bravery against a syren plant, Sirra expressed her doubts that the young Jedi Knights would last even five minutes down in the forest underlevels. Their Force powers would not keep them safe, she asserted, if this was how they used them.

Lowie fixed his sister with a challenging look, trying to explain difficult concepts. His friends were merely "exercising" their abilities. Learning and practice were never wasted. He insisted that his friends were much stronger than they appeared.

Sirra shrugged away the comment and began pacing the flat, sun-drenched platform again. Exasperated, Lowie demanded to know how she expected him to help her solve her problem.

Surprise registered on Sirra's face. She hadn't *asked* him for a solution.

It was Lowie's turn to be perplexed. If he

saw his sister confused or in pain, he asked, shouldn't he assume she wanted help?

Sirra's eyes narrowed. With a quick series of gruff words, she reminded him of when he had fallen down a few minutes earlier and bruised his . . . his *dignity*. Had he wanted anyone to solve his problem for him?

Lowie shook his head. Sirra raised her eyebrows, asking if now he understood.

Lowie saw what his sister was getting at, but that had not been the same thing. He *knew* she needed help.

Sirra sat down again at the platform's edge, looking out across the wroshyr trees. Lowie squatted beside his sister with earnest concern, and her expression softened. She didn't want him to solve her problem, she said, but that didn't mean he wasn't helping.

Lowie realized that it was helping her just to have someone who listened.

He clasped her shoulder, and Sirra sat closer to him. For now, that seemed to be enough.

7

FROM HER UNUSUAL perch, Jaina surveyed the high-tech tree city and realized how much Kashyyyk looked like an organic version of Coruscant.

Here at the canopy level, surrounded by industrial structures and Wookiee living quarters, Jaina saw tall exhaust ports and crystalline windows that reflected the hazy gray-white sky. The crowns of tall trees thrust above the main canopy like skyscraper towers covered with foliage. A huge clump of majestic growth in the distance sat like an island above the leafy waves of the unbroken treetops; from this distance, it reminded her of the pyramidal towers of the Imperial Palace.

Jaina thought with a twinge of homesickness that she missed her mother. The last time she and Jacen had returned to the capital world, though, they had lost their friend Zekk, who had been captured by the Shadow Academy. . . .

Clusters of Wookiee homes dotted the canopy, compact dwellings connected to the computer factory complex by natural roadways that extended like the spokes of a wheel across the treetops. Imported banthas trudged along the wide, wooden roads, brushing against encroaching leaves. They plodded along sturdy worn branches hundreds of meters above the untraveled and treacherous lower levels of the primeval forest.

The bantha Jaina and her friends rode from Lowie's home to the computer fabrication complex was large enough that all five companions could ride on the padded seats strapped to the beast's back. The bantha had a rich, spicy animal scent that tingled in her nostrils. A harness made of bright red ribbons jingled with burnished brass bells.

Her brother Jacen patted the wiry cinnamon-brown fur of the enormous beast of burden. Riding this bantha seemed to be the most enjoyable part of their trip for him so far. The driver, a mousy Sullustan with huge dark eyes that glinted in the sunlight, hunched between the enormous ridged horns that curved around the bantha's head. The docile beast moved along the wooden walkway, paying no heed to the lush vegetation on all sides.

"Banthas were bred for desert travel," Jacen piped up, "but this guy seems to love it here."

Indeed, Jaina thought, the beast seemed fat and healthy, content to carry passengers from the residential districts to the main fabrication facility. They passed other Wookiees walking to work, eating up the distance with long-legged strides.

Beside her on the padded riding structure, Tenel Ka stared ahead, her expression unreadable but alert, ready for anything. Lowie and Sirra sat on the back cushions, chatting comfortably in the Wookiee language.

Jaina looked forward to her tour of the computer factory. She couldn't wait to see the engineering marvels and industrial facilities the Wookiees had installed on their wilderness world. Lowie probably would have been eager as well, if he hadn't been so concerned about his sister.

The bantha stopped and let them off at an outer checkpoint that gave access to the technical complex. Using handholds on the padded seats, the companions climbed down the hairy back of the bantha and jumped to the interlocked wooden deck. Since the bantha transportation systems were designed for use by tall Wookiees, the drop was a meter longer than Jaina expected. She wondered how the diminutive Sullustan driver ever managed to climb his way onto the beast's head.

Lowie paid the driver a few credit chips, and the bantha trudged back down the cleared arboreal highway toward the residential islands in search of new passengers.

Jaina looked at the multiplatformed industrial facility, seeing decks mounted in tiers on the uppermost branches. Lowie growled in excitement and pointed to a level platform high above and behind them. From this angle, Jaina couldn't see anything on its surface, but then a small craft rose with a grating roar of supercharged sublight engines.

"That's an old Y-wing," she said, recognizing the outdated designs of the craft. The Y-wing had a triangular cockpit flanked by two long engine pods that together gave the fighter its characteristic shape like the letter for which it had been named. This starfighter had been refurbished and upgraded, and its engines were loud and powerful. The craft's afterburners kicked in behind the engine pods, and the Y-wing streaked into the skies of Kashyyyk.

Another identical starfighter rose from the

platform, hovered for a moment as the pilot adjusted the controls, then streaked off after its companion. A third and a fourth Y-wing also soared away.

"How many of them are there?" Jacen asked.

Jaina watched in admiration. "Probably an entire squadron," she suggested, then suddenly remembered something she had heard. "The New Republic needs all the military strength it can get if we're going to fight the Second Imperium. We don't have time to build all new ships, so I think they're refurbishing the old ones that have been mothballed since the fall of the Emperor."

"What do you mean, refurbishing?" Jacen asked.

"Well, there's nothing actually *wrong* with the old Y-wings," Jaina said with a shrug. "They were great fighters during the Rebellion, but with new technology we can modernize the engines, increase their hyperdrive multipliers. Since we're on Kashyyyk, I'll bet they're getting new navicomputers, guidance and tactical systems, and central processors installed."

Lowie and Sirra nodded their shaggy heads vigorously to show that Jaina was right. She looked into the sky and watched as, one after another, Y-wings shot upward in a spectacular aerial display.

Sirra said something else, and Em Teedee translated. "Mistress Sirra suggests we remain here to watch, since the upgraded ships often test their new systems. She assures us it is quite a breathtaking sight." Lowie bellowed in agreement. Jaina wanted nothing more than to witness the demonstration.

When twelve of the ships had been launched into the air, circling over the treetop industrial facility, they flew in tight formation, one behind the other, a chain of powerful spacecraft. Their engines boomed like distant thunder through the upper atmosphere. The pilots followed their leader, swooping down, cracking the whip in the sky.

The Y-wings formed convoluted figure eights, flying so close to each other that their hulls were almost kissing. But the new guidance systems and engines did not fail them. The refurbished Y-wings performed flawlessly, and Jaina felt a warm satisfaction inside. She held her breath, amazed.

If Qorl and the Second Imperium could see this demonstration, she mused, they might think twice before attempting to tackle the New Republic.

From one of the connecting structures that

linked the perimeter platform to the central levels of the fabrication facility, a door dilated open. An excessively tall, spindly droid appeared, its legs like thin support pipes, its long arms coppery. The droid had a squarish head with rounded corners and optical sensors mounted on all sides. It strutted out, moving with spidery grace as it balanced round footpads on the deck.

"Greetings, honored guests," the tall droid said, weaving on its leg hinges as it walked. "I am the Tour Droid, happy to serve you this morning. I have received instructions to give you the complete tour of our facilities—in fact, the expanded VIP tour. I will speak Basic, unless you prefer to converse in Wookiee, Sullustan, Bothan, or another native language."

Jaina shook her head. "Basic will do fine, thanks."

The Tour Droid turned a pirouette on one long rodlike leg, and Jaina guessed that the droid had been constructed so tall in order to comfortably accommodate speaking with Wookiees.

The droid strode ahead with a mantislike gait. "You've already seen our air show for this morning," it said. "Now for the good stuff."

Since Jaina loved learning about the way things functioned, every workstation inside the fabrication facility intrigued her. Interesting smells of lubricants, cryogens, and electrical solder surrounded her. The air was filled with buzzing, humming sounds against a background of white noise from thousands of complicated manufacturing labs.

Jaina looked to the ceiling high above their heads and saw embedded glowpanels that suffused the corridors with a constant white light. At regular intervals, where hallways intersected, they passed trapdoor hatches that provided access to the underside of the factory and emergency evacuation routes down into the lower forest levels.

The Tour Droid led the group into a room full of transparent cylinders that stretched from floor to ceiling, pillars filled with a bubbling fluid and sparkling diamondlike matrices.

"Here you see our crystal-growing tanks," the droid said, raising the volume of its speaker patch to drown out the gurgling noises and whir of air-recirculation fans. "In these carefully modulated tanks we send electrical impulses in specific currents through the nutrient fluid to distribute crystalline molecules in solution. This encourages them to grow into a precise matrix with facet angles and electronic pathways mapped for our galaxy-renowned computer cores. A building is only as strong as its foundation, and these crystalline cores form the critical foundation of our computer architecture."

Jacen rubbed his fingers against a curved tank, tracing the paths of tiny bubbles as they rose toward the ceiling. "This is neat," he said.

"Please don't touch the cylinders," the Tour Droid said. "Faint electrostatic discharges from your body could disturb the crystallization processes inside."

Jacen pulled his hand away and looked sheepishly at his sister. She didn't bother to chide him for it, though, since she had wanted to do the same thing herself.

The next room was exceedingly cold, with puffs of white steam curling around the door frame. The air smelled of scoured metal and frost. Inside, robotic arms moved about, sloshing thin metallic wafers through baths of liquid oxygen, pools of ultracold fluid that halted any contaminants from spreading across the surface. "These wafers are delicate circuit boards," the Tour Droid said, "a perfectly pure substrate on which we pattern complex memory maps."

Jaina drew a long frigid breath, blinking her eyes. Even with their thick Wookiee fur, Lowie and Sirra shivered, though Tenel Ka in her scanty reptilian armor displayed no sign of discomfort. "Fascinating," she said.

The Tour Droid turned and, with long scarecrowish strides, led them through the cold room. The next chamber was large and bustling, filled with hardworking Wookiees, each wearing a mesh bodysuit made of fine wires that held their fur in place. White cloth masks covered the lower halves of their hairy faces.

The workers looked up and chuffed greetings to the visitors. Lowie waved, recognizing his mother at her workstation. Kallabow nodded, blinking her eyes in their whorls of dark fur, then bent back to her tasks, carefully concentrating on the circuits.

"For the past few months our workers have logged extralong shifts and odd hours to meet the heavy quotas necessary to prepare our defense against the Second Imperium," the Tour Droid said. "Here the Wookiees are installing finished chips. The mesh suits you see them wearing are electrostatic screens to prevent even the faintest stray foreign particles from drifting into the air. Any contamination could be disastrous, since these components are so complex."

"I can believe it," Jaina said.

The Wookiee technicians bent over their workstations, using delicate forceps and tweezers to remove minuscule chips patterned and cut from the large glittering wafers they had just seen in the cryogenic lab.

"These basic designs are used for many different systems," the Tour Droid said. "While our specialties are in tactical systems, central guidance computers, and mainframe system controls, some of our chips are used in sophisticated droid models. Most droids are manufactured on robotic industrial worlds, however, such as Mechis III."

"Oh my, did he say *droids*?" Em Teedee chirped. "Do you suppose any of my components might have been manufactured here?"

Lowie rumbled a comment, and Jaina nodded. "Chewbacca helped put you together, Em Teedee. I suspect that lots of your components came from here."

"Oh dear, you don't think he used defective or rejected parts, do you?" Em Teedee asked. Lowie chuffed with laughter, and the little droid scolded him. "My question was entirely serious, Master Lowbacca."

After they walked through the chamber,

Em Teedee continued to exhibit his curiosity. "Master Lowbacca, would you mind turning around so that I can see the entire room? If this is my birthplace, I'd like to give it a good look. . . . How fascinating!"

Lowie obliged, turning his waist so that the small translating droid's optical sensors could record every detail. "And I thought this trip was going to be dull," Em Teedee said. "This is ever so much more interesting than those dangerous adventures you insist on having."

For the end of their tour the long-legged droid took them to the highest platform in the entire facility, the transportation control and shipping tower, a computer-filled room with workstations so high off the floor they were at Jaina's eye level where she couldn't easily reach them. Several Wookiees stood around the stations, gazing up through the transparent dome overhead. The dome was reinforced with support girders that crisscrossed in triangular patterns against the hazy sunlight shining down.

"Because we are such a busy commercial facility," the Tour Droid said, "a constant stream of space traffic comes through this complex. Here we verify every incoming transport craft to make certain we receive no unwelcome visitors. We also have security monitoring satellites in orbit, ready to defend Kashyyyk, once they receive orders from the control tower."

The Wookiee traffic controllers worked as a team, communication headsets mounted to their shaggy heads and voice pickups clamped to their throats. They did not divert their attention even for a moment as the visitors entered.

Before the Tour Droid could continue, Chewbacca strode in, accompanied by Lowie and Sirra's father, Mahraccor. Mahraccor waved at his children; his dark streak of fur stood out much like Lowie's. Chewbacca bellowed a greeting and held out a large misshapen object, a blackened device that had once been a polished, precisely angled crystal.

"That's the *Shadow Chaser*'s computer core," Jaina said.

Chewbacca nodded vigorously and spoke low growling words.

"Chewbacca and Mahraccor here say they have been searching for you children," said the Tour Droid.

"Excuse me," Em Teedee chimed in, "but *I* serve as the translator droid here. Master Chewbacca, after returning from a pleasant visit with his family, has removed the *Shadow Chaser*'s damaged navicomputer central processor core. As you can see, he has spoken with Master Mahraccor, and they have successfully located the suitable replacement components to get the ship up and running again. Hooray!"

Chewie pointed to the burned pathways on the *Shadow Chaser*'s removed navicomputer core. Lowie's father also spoke up, and Em Teedee said, "Master Mahraccor asserts that this is an exciting new design, an Imperial configuration he has never seen before. Fortunately, however, he is confident that the facilities here on Kashyyyk can repair it quite nicely."

The Tour Droid bent over on its long, stretched-out body. "You are quite good at translating Wookiee speech, my colleague," it said, "but you lack the finesse for being a true Tour Droid. You seem not to have the ability to make interesting comparisons that customers can understand. For instance, you might have said, 'With our facilities here we can place this damaged core in one of our crystal baths, flush out the impurities and the carbon scoring, and use our own master computers to retrace the circuits and map the electronic pathways. In short, we will provide a bacta tank to heal the computer core.'"

Em Teedee wasn't impressed. "They certainly didn't *need* to hear all of that. Of course, I wouldn't presume to tell you *your* job," he said. "We have more important things to do."

The Tour Droid did not respond to the insult, since he had no doubt been given thorough programming in tactfulness.

"Thank you for the tour," Jaina said. "It was very interesting."

The Tour Droid stood up straighter, and the optical sensors mounted on all sides of its boxy head brightened with pleasure. "That is the finest compliment you could have given me, Mistress Jaina Solo."

8

SURROUNDED BY DIMNESS in his private office, lit only by recorded starlight from distant parts of the galaxy, Brakiss contemplated the plans of the Second Imperium.

Time slipped away from him as he allowed himself to be swallowed up in thoughts. Possibilities for conquest engrossed him, and he ran them over and over in his head, contemplating the complete destruction of the Rebels and his former mentor, Luke Skywalker. Such imaginings soothed him. Resting his elbows on the polished black desk, Brakiss touched his fingertips together and smiled.

Suddenly, a startling signal destroyed his concentration like a thunderbolt. The potent alarm pulsed again, and he used his much-needed Jedi skills to calm himself. "This is Brakiss," he responded.

"Qorl here," a voice replied. An image appeared on the flatscreen communicator built into his desk. The old TIE pilot seemed rattled—and that surprised Brakiss even more than the alarm had. Qorl was one of the steadiest officers in the Second Imperium.

"We have a coded message coming into the Shadow Academy, sir. It carries the highest level of encryption. Every marking indicates that the transmission is of the utmost importance. You must receive the message yourself and respond personally."

Brakiss blinked. "Any indication of the sender's identity?" His thoughts whirled. Tamith Kai and Zekk had already departed on their mission to Kashyyyk, but even they were incapable of sending such a high-level message.

"No indication, sir," Qorl said, "but I would recommend that you respond without delay."

"I'm on my way," Brakiss said, and switched off, propelling himself out of his chair in one fluid motion.

He raced through the curved metallic corridors, taking an automated lift platform to the transmitting and receiving tower, which contained the machinery that cast a cloaking field around the spike-ringed station.

Several stormtroopers stood alert as Brakiss swept into the transmitting tower. Qorl worked at the receiving stations, scanning computerized readouts and recording the coded signal. Brakiss noted that the man used his biological right hand, letting his bulky robotic limb hang motionless at his side. Qorl blinked at the Shadow Academy leader. "They have begun transmitting again, Lord Brakiss," he said. "They seem to be quite impatient."

"All right, let's input the decryption routine." Standing beside Qorl, Brakiss had to think for a moment to summon the correct string of symbols and numbers, then keyed in his password so that the Shadow Academy computers could translate the high-level coded message.

Qorl handed Brakiss a dangling headset. "The message is for your ears only. Listen on this channel." Qorl helped Brakiss mount the earphones and microphone snugly against his head.

Brakiss listened to the crackle of static as the convoluted message ran through its code-deciphering algorithms and finally resolved itself into coherent words. The voice pounded against his eardrums, harsh, almost reptilian, dripping with evil.

Brakiss's eyes widened, and fear drove a spike through his mind. He cleared his throat twice before he could respond. "Yes, my lord," he finally answered. "Yes, at once." He drew a deep breath to continue, but the sender terminated the signal. Brakiss heard only static.

He stood rigid, using all of his Jedi strengths to keep himself from trembling. Qorl waited beside him, leathery face emotionless, his eyes unblinking. Only a slight furrow across the TIE pilot's forehead showed how concerned he was.

Brakiss spoke quietly, looking at Qorl but knowing that the stormtrooper guards were also listening intently. "The Emperor," he said hoarsely, "the Emperor is coming here!"

An ominous transport shuttle dropped out of hyperspace in the vicinity of the Shadow Academy. The shuttle was an Imperial design, the Emperor's private escort ship, armored with tarnished hull plates. Its configuration was similar to a triangular *Lambda*-class transport, except that this craft bore very special weaponry, sensing devices, and ultrapowerful hyperdrive engines. Even such extreme modifications, though, were of little consequence when compared to the importance of the passenger it carried.

Brakiss stood within the hangar bay, struggling to drive back his anxiety. In all this time he had never met the Emperor face-to-face, despite his unwavering service to the Second Imperium.

The Great Leader of the Second Imperium, Emperor Palpatine, must somehow have escaped death years earlier—though Brakiss had been sure the Emperor had been destroyed . . . several times, in fact. He did not know what secret Palpatine had used, or how he had managed to restore himself to life, but Brakiss didn't care—all that mattered was that the Second Imperium was in the most capable hands imaginable.

The comm buzzed and Qorl's voice made an announcement. "Lord Brakiss, the Emperor's private transport has just come out of hyperspace. I await your orders."

Brakiss leaned closer to the wall speaker. "Very well, drop the Shadow Academy's cloaking field and transmit our greetings to Emperor Palpatine. We are honored by his visit."

"Yes, sir," Qorl said, signing off.

Brakiss could feel no difference, not even through the Force, as the invisibility shield dissolved around the station. He stood with an honor guard of stormtroopers inside the cleared docking bay. The transparent atmosphere containment field flickered.

Brakiss stared out into open space, watching the awesome craft approach. The stormtroopers stood more rigidly, their armor locking into place, boots clicking together.

The Emperor's transport followed Qorl's signal. The three-bladed shuttle glided through the atmosphere containment field, which flickered and sparked as it folded around the hull of the ship. The Imperial transport coasted to the center of the broad deck, then lowered itself to a stable position.

Brakiss swallowed a large lump in his throat. He transmitted to Qorl. "Reactivate the cloaking shield, please—we don't want to expose ourselves any longer than necessary."

"It is done, sir," Qorl said.

The stormtroopers shouldered their weapons and stood in perfect ranks. Brakiss stepped forward to offer greeting, but paused when nothing happened. The Emperor's transport remained silent except for a few hissing and ticking sounds as the ship settled. He saw no movement inside. The hatch remained stubbornly shut. Brakiss waited for any sign.

Finally, a voice boomed from loudspeakers mounted outside the Emperor's shuttle. "Attention, all Shadow Academy personnel! The Emperor has arrived. As a security precaution, we insist that everyone depart the docking bay immediately. The Emperor has a private escort of Imperial guards and wishes no further contact at this time."

The announcement took Brakiss completely by surprise. When he noticed that his mouth was hanging open in foolish astonishment, he closed it so quickly that his teeth clicked together. The Emperor had come to the Shadow Academy—and now Palpatine refused Brakiss's honor escort. The Great Leader wanted to be left *alone*?

Brakiss realized that he had hesitated in following Palpatine's instructions. Aghast and trying to make up for lost time, he turned and clapped his hands smartly. "You heard the orders! Everyone, about-face. Clear the docking bay. The Emperor wishes his privacy."

The stormtroopers turned and, with a booming clatter on the metal deck, marched out of the docking bay and into the curved corridors.

"Sir," one of the stormtroopers said, breaking ranks to stop in front of Brakiss, "I had requested to be part of the Emperor's personal escort squad. I'll stay here to greet him as he disembarks."

Brakiss blinked in shock, noting the stormtrooper's service number. He recognized Qorl's trainee, Norys. Qorl had said the burly young man was ambitious and ill-tempered, but

Brakiss was nonetheless stunned at the impertinence.

"You will follow my orders, trooper," Brakiss snapped. "The Second Imperium has no room for those who don't understand discipline." He drew in a cold breath. "If I see any further instance of your failure to obey commands, you will be ejected from the airlock into space. Is that understood?"

As Norys clomped off without acknowledging Brakiss's rebuff, the master of the Shadow Academy turned to look back at the silent Imperial shuttle. He himself was unable to comprehend why the Emperor had come here if he had no intention of interacting with the Shadow Academy, or at least meeting with Brakiss personally.

However, the Emperor was the ultimate master, and Brakiss would not dare question Palpatine's orders.

The last one to leave the docking bay, he turned with a swirl of his silvery robes and stepped outside before transmitting the signal that closed and sealed the doors to the docking bay.

As he stood in the outer corridor, though, Brakiss made a decision of his own. He was master of this station—and was required to know what happened aboard it, wasn't he?

He had followed the Emperor's wishes to the letter, but now he needed to see what was going on. Brakiss went to a videomonitor designed for observation of docking and loading procedures.

With the docking bay emptied of stormtroopers and Shadow Academy representatives, the hatches finally opened on the Emperor's shuttle. On the monitor Brakiss was impressed to see four Imperial guards stride out, shrouded in scarlet robes. The intimidating red guards had been the most feared elite corps of Palpatine's forces, and now four of them had accompanied the Emperor here. Smooth red armor covered their heads and shoulders like cowls, reminding him of historical images he had seen of ancient Mandalorian uniforms.

The red Imperial guards moved away from the ship and took up defensive positions, their robes flowing like flames around them. A shudder ran down Brakiss's spine. He tried to feel the intense dark force crackling from the core of the Imperial transport ship. The Emperor, he knew, must be in there somewhere.

Through the voice pickup mounted in the docking bay, Brakiss heard a clanking, slamming sound. Two pairs of squat, powerful worker droids tromped down the wide extended ramp, carrying an enormously heavy isolation chamber. The worker droids, little more than the powerful arms and legs mounted on a stocky body core, hauled their burden without complaint.

The droids were gentle with their cargo, moving smoothly, carefully, despite the immense power in their hydraulic limbs. They carried the huge tank off the Imperial ship and into the docking bay. Side panels on the isolation chamber's black riveted walls blinked with multicolored lights; computer displays showed life monitors and external communications.

The four red guards surrounded the chamber, looking protective and menacing. Then they marched toward the broad doors—two in front of the chamber, two behind—into the main core of the Shadow Academy.

Brakiss hurried to open the doors for them, but somehow the computer-locked seals were automatically broken before he could do so. The doors slammed open, as if controlled by the Emperor's dark side powers.

The red guards strode forward, still surrounding the worker droids. The huge isolation tank hissed and buzzed and bleeped as a thousand electronic systems monitored its supremely important occupant.

Brakiss stopped in front of the foremost pair of Imperial guards. "Greetings. I am Master Brakiss of the Shadow Academy."

The leader of the red guards turned his armored head, and Brakiss felt a cold scrutiny through the black eyeslit. "You will leave us alone. We have important work, and we require privacy. You may guide us to our chambers—and then leave."

Brakiss could barely contain his dismay. "But . . . I am the Master of the Shadow Academy."

The red guard said, "And the Emperor is the master of the galaxy. He wishes privacy for now. We suggest that you do not displease him."

Brakiss backed away, bowing quickly. "I have no wish to displease the Emperor. Forgive my impudence."

After Brakiss indicated the quarters to which the visitors had been assigned—the plushest and most spacious accommodations aboard the station—the red guards and worker droids marched into the chambers, leaving Brakiss alone out in the corridor.

He felt belittled, insignificant, stepped on, as if all of his accomplishments and work meant nothing to the Emperor. It baffled him. What could be the purpose of it? He frowned as thoughts whirled inside his head.

The Emperor had originally died in the destruction of the second Death Star, but six years after his defeat, Palpatine had been resurrected in a series of clones, which had also—presumably—been destroyed.

Now, after observing the isolation tank, the secrecy, the inexplicable behavior of the four Imperial guards, Brakiss felt a new and deeper fear coil through his body. He wondered if something could be wrong, if the Emperor could perhaps be in failing health again. . . .

If that was the case, the Second Imperium was indeed in great trouble.

9

AS A FORMER TIE pilot, Qorl had been trained in the Imperial way, with loyalties and duties and responses drilled into him. No questions, only orders. His mind had been programmed to turn him into a perfect fighting machine for the Empire.

The cornerstone of that training had been *discipline*. And one thing Qorl knew: the young man who stood before him was not disciplined.

He wondered if perhaps Brakiss and Tamith Kai had been too hasty in accepting Norys and his band of young ruffians from Coruscant to be trained as stormtroopers and pilots. True, the battles ahead to recapture lost glory, to reclaim stolen territory, would require every set of capable hands for the Second Imperium. But even if Qorl did manage to turn the rest of the Lost Ones gang into serviceable troopers and pilots, this one was *trouble*.

At the control pad of the simulation chamber, Qorl programmed in a new set of targets while Norys recharged his blaster rifle. He vowed to train this one, and *keep* training him, until he saw some genuine progress in the ambitious fighter.

"I still say I should have been sent on the raid with Tamith Kai," Norys grumbled, waving his weapon as if it made him feel more secure. "I could have taken out a few enemies, evened the score a little bit for our side. Set a few of those big Wookiee trees on fire."

Qorl set the simulated targets in rapid motion: black, orange, and blue for Rebels, and white for stormtroopers. "It's a small raid," Qorl said. "Zekk is directing the troops. There was no need for a second leader."

Norys took aim at a blue target and missed. He liked target practice better when the targets were slow simulations like mynocks. It was fun to kill them. "Then they should have sent me alone, old man. I'm a better leader now than that trash collector will ever be."

Trouble, Qorl thought, *definitely trouble.* "Why do you say that?"

"Because," Norys said, taking aim at an orange target, but only nicking the edge of it, "my followers are so afraid of me they'd never *dare* disobey my orders." He missed once more. "Is the aim-point on this blaster offset again?"

"You aren't concentrating on your target," Qorl said, then addressed the candidate's comment in a neutral tone. "Your example is indeed one method of leadership. But you have much to learn."

Norys bristled and missed another shot. He rounded on the former TIE pilot with a menacing growl. "Like what, old man?"

Qorl didn't flinch or back down. He had faced tougher adversaries than this young bully—though perhaps none with such pure mean-spiritedness. "You could learn to concentrate on your weapon and shut out distractions. You could also learn how to aim and hit your intended target each time, rather than just talking about it," Qorl pointed out. "The way you are shooting today, you would have become a casualty in only a few seconds in a real firefight."

"Really, old man?" Norys's lips pulled back in something between a snarl and a grin. He turned back toward the targets and, moving his blaster rifle in a slow semicircle, flooded the area with blaster bolts, never removing his finger from the firing stud. When he was finished, every target had registered a hit. A complete slaughter. Norys turned back toward Qorl with a satisfied smirk. "How much more target practice do I need, old man?"

"Enough practice so you don't destroy our own troops during a raid," Qorl replied.

Norys shrugged. "We all make a few sacrifices to meet our goals." He glanced back at the targets. "Seems like a fair trade-off to me." He tossed the spent blaster rifle at Qorl, who caught it with his good arm.

Trouble, Qorl thought, *definitely trouble*.

10

STARS BURNED IN the midnight sky like a billion white-hot embers on a slab of black marble. Jacen, Jaina, and Tenel Ka had long since retired to their beds—but Lowie couldn't sleep. Perched comfortably on the wide railing of the upper verandah, with the simmering night sounds of the forest all around him, he kept a watchful eye on his sister's window.

Sirra still insisted she wanted to imitate Lowie's feat with the syren plant, and he could not talk her out of it. Now he feared she would leave him behind at the last moment, go alone on her dangerous quest—as Raaba had done. So far, though, he had seen no sign that his sister was planning anything so foolish.

Because of increased production quotas for the New Republic's military requirements, their parents had both volunteered to work the night shift at the computer fabrication facility. Kallabow and Mahraccor had spent

their lives at their jobs, contented if somewhat unchallenged, and seemed baffled that
neither of their children wanted to follow in
their footsteps.

But Sirra demanded constant challenges,
and went out of her way to create some when
life didn't provide her with enough of them.

The light in Sirra's room shimmered like a
warm fire behind the window's leafy shade.
Small glowing mesh cages rested outside her
window and on various platforms throughout
the Wookiee residential district—containers
filled with a sweet-smelling substance that
proved an irresistible attractant to a species
of tiny glowing gnats called phosfleas. When
the cages were placed outside, clusters of the
harmless phosphorescent insects swarmed
around them to provide a natural, pollution-
free light source.

Sitting alone outside under the starlight,
Lowie had watched Sirra's shadowy figure
moving about in her room, pacing as if agi-
tated, but he had seen no sign of her for some
time now. Perhaps his sister was trying to
sleep, he thought.

But though vague foreboding crackled like
static through his mind, he liked being alone in
the restful darkness, high above the ground,
where he could think. It felt good to be home on

Kashyyyk. He drew in a lungful of the wood-scented air and practiced a Jedi relaxation technique, slowly willing his tense muscles to unknot—

—only to jump a meter into the air as a set of cold claws pricked his back. Lowie stumbled to his feet and spun toward the railing, his defensive Wookiee instincts coming into play.

Sirra, shaking with silent laughter, hauled herself up over the railing onto the verandah and resheathed her claws, complimenting him on his reflexes. At least, she said, he had convinced her that he might be of some help during her quest. Lowie groaned, trying to quell the surge of adrenaline. He asked her if the surprise had been designed strictly to test him.

Sirra's voice grew more serious, and she lowered her head. She had wanted to demonstrate that she could slip off alone, if she wanted, and Lowie wouldn't have been able to stop her. Sirra turned her head up so that the starlight gleamed on the pattern-shaved tufts of her fur. Then she looked at her brother and promised that she wouldn't go without him.

Lowie reseated himself on the railing and

gazed up at the stars. He grumbled about the unexpected ways she made her points.

Sirra purred, thanking him for the odd compliment, making herself comfortable beside him.

Lowie grunted, not sure he had intended his remark as praise, but the fact that Sirra was pleased by the comment spoke volumes. She enjoyed being different, just as her friend Raaba had. . . .

As if sensing the direction of his thoughts, Sirra began talking about Raaba, how the sleek, dark Wookiee had loved the stars. Even when they were small, the two young females used to sneak out at night and watch the skies for hours.

Lowie's shoulders slumped. Raaba should not have died. She had taken a foolish risk, going alone.

Sirra growled, pointing out that Lowie had taken exactly the same risk.

Lowie barked in agreement—yes indeed, he had been a fool.

His sister's voice was harsh. If he had it to do again, would he do anything different? Would he take a friend?

Lowie nodded a quick affirmative. Sirra said nothing, but even in the darkness Lowie could see her fur bristling in disbelief. After a long silence he finally sighed, then shook his head.

After another long pause Sirra told her brother how much Raaba admired him, how much she had wanted to be like Lowie.

Lowie looked up at the sky again, at the stars that Raaba had loved. He gave a questioning growl. When he had left for the Jedi academy, Lowie and Raaba had been too young to speak of making a life-bond. He still had his Jedi training ahead of him . . . and Raaba had plans too. With Sirra.

Here Sirra's voice broke. She crooned a low mournful note and then another. After a time, Lowie added his voice to hers, and together beneath the stars, they poured out their grief for a lost friend.

Hours later, Lowie felt more refreshed than he would have thought possible, even had he slept the entire night. It had been better to spend the time growing closer to his sister.

Sirra's husky voice broke into his thoughts, asking about his Jedi friends. Would they grieve for him, if he were gone? Like she and Lowie had done for Raaba?

He nodded emphatically, and she told him he was fortunate to have found them.

Encouraged, he asked her more about the plans she and Raaba had made.

Sirra did not speak for so long he was afraid he had offended her or reopened an old wound. Finally she described how they were going to be pilots, galactic adventurers. They had planned to work on freighters until they earned enough credits to buy their own ship and explore the stars. They could have been rich traders. She chuffed with bitter laughter. Raaba even had some fur-brained notion that they could make their names by charting out new hyperspace routes.

Lowie's fur bristled, and he commented that such a career was a dangerous business.

Sirra's tone was wry, pointing out that danger had never deterred their friend Raaba. Sirra spread her hands, confessing that she didn't want to do that anymore. Not without Raaba. She didn't know what she wanted to do now—but she definitely didn't want to stay on Kashyyyk.

Sirra paused again and stared upward. Lowie followed his sister's gaze, wondering if she imagined Raaba out there among the stars, exploring and having the adventures the two of them had always dreamed of.

Sirra sighed. It was difficult to lose a friend, she said.

Lowie realized how easy it was to take friends—and family—for granted. He found it hard to imagine how lonely his sister must be.

Sirra hesitantly asked him if he would spend the day with her while Chewbacca and Jaina continued to tinker with the *Shadow Chaser*.

Remembering his earlier feeling of foreboding, Lowie gladly agreed.

11

AS MIDMORNING SUNSHINE drove off the last shreds of mist that clung to the wroshyr treetops, four muscular Wookiees marched to the transportation control tower of the computer fabrication complex.

The four looked just like any other Wookiees dressed appropriately for work in the high-tech factory. They were tall and powerful and carried no visible weapons. The newcomers punched in the correct access codes and passed into the high-security tower that rose high above the other tree platforms. Their timing was perfect for the morning shift change.

When they crossed the checkpoint station into the control tower, the four passed an electrostatic air-filtration grid. The images of the four Wookiees flickered in the unseen discharge, just for an instant, before their appearance restored itself.

No one noticed.

The real Wookiees who had been assigned to the next shift lay stunned inside a small supply chamber in an outer storage platform. The Wookiees on duty, weary from hours of monitoring the ships that came and went from the computer facility, were happy to finish their shift and return home. They signed off their stations and handed over the equipment to the new crew, who gruffly acknowledged them in synthesized Wookiee grunts and growls.

The earlier crew departed, leaving the facility's control points, the lockout systems, and Kashyyyk's satellite defense functions in the hands of the newcomers.

One of the new Wookiees sealed the control tower door, pulled out a concealed blaster, then melted the alarm systems and intruder detection devices. Sparks flew. Metal and plasteel dripped, smoldering black. All four Wookiees then touched their waists, switching off the hidden holographic generators belted there. Their images shimmered, dissolving away, to reveal a commando team from the Shadow Academy.

"The holo-disguises worked perfectly," Zekk said, brushing at his leather armor and straightening his crimson-lined cape, happy to be himself again.

The stormtrooper stationed at the door said, "Alarm systems disengaged. No problems here."

The other two infiltrators, the Nightsisters Tamith Kai and Vonnda Ra, stood before the complex computer systems. The Wookiee-level panels forced them to reach up to use the controls. Vonnda Ra craned her neck to examine the readouts and identify systems.

Tamith Kai brooded, mulling over various details. She clasped her long-nailed hands together. "This plan must proceed according to schedule," she said. "If it does, it looks as if success will be ours."

"We'll succeed," Zekk said confidently. "I won't disappoint Master Brakiss."

Vonnda Ra worked at two of the control panels, studying keyboards and diagnostics. Satisfied, the Nightsister slipped an insulated vibroblade from her belt sheath and flicked on the humming knife. She bent down under the panels and slashed sideways to sever the power cords. Bright sparks spat out, followed by curling white electrical smoke.

She backed away, covering her nose against the acrid smell, then stood up straight again, looking satisfied. "Kashyyyk's orbital defense systems have been permanently disabled."

Zekk nodded at the destroyed control panel, his green eyes flashing. "Sure looks permanent to me."

"You're in command of this mission, Zekk," Tamith Kai said, plugging a hand-held translator into the communications console. "Don't you think it's time you transmitted your signal to lure those Jedi brats here, where we can take care of them?" The Nightsister looked insufferably pleased with herself.

Zekk swallowed, his mind whirling. He had known this moment would come, and he had to face it.

"Do I sense hesitation?" Tamith Kai snapped.

"No," he answered, "just working out the proper wording for the message. They must be intrigued and concerned . . . and convinced."

Zekk hovered over the communications console, pondering his words, then punched them into the translator that would convert them to the appropriate Wookiee dialect and send a text message with the highest priority to where Jacen and Jaina were staying with their friends.

If he worded it correctly, he knew the twins would come.

• • •

Back in the Wookiee home high in the trees, Jacen did his best to keep up with his friends in the fast-paced computer skill game. But the other players—Lowie, Sirra, and Tenel Ka—far outmatched his reflexes. Jaina, meanwhile, had gone with Chewbacca to work on their damaged ship.

The friends sat at the four sides of a rectangular control grid, each with one hand on the small, flexible motion sensors that guided tiny laserprojected simulations of space fighters. They fought a miniature reenactment of the original Death Star battle.

Lowie and Sirra flew fast X-wing fighters, while Jacen and Tenel Ka were stuck with flanking defensive ships, sluggish old Y-wings. The computer did its best to pursue them all, its simulated TIE fighters firing repeatedly, while enormous turbolaser cannons emplaced in the Death Star trench crisscrossed space with deadly fire-lines.

Jacen was good at target shooting; he and Jaina had often used the *Millennium Falcon*'s quad laser cannons to blast chunks of space debris out of Coruscant orbit. But Lowie and his sister were more intimately familiar with complex computer games, and

Tenel Ka had the finely honed reflexes of a warrior from Dathomir.

Jacen's fingers flew across his motion sensor, banking his Y-wing—but a TIE fighter clung close to his rear engine pods. Jacen spun about. "Hey, get off my back," he cried. By sheer luck, the TIE fighter crossed into one of the turbolaser blasts from the trench guns, conveniently saving Jacen.

Anxious to divert attention from his so-so performance in the game, Jacen tried to distract the other players in the most obvious way. Between spins and banks and firing, he told a joke.

"Hey, guys, do you know what sound Whiphids make when they kiss?"

"I have neither seen nor heard Whiphids kiss," Tenel Ka said.

"Master Lowbacca says he's certain he would never wish to," Em Teedee said.

"Come on," Jacen interrupted. "It's a joke. What sound do Whiphids make when they kiss?" He paused a second, cocking an eyebrow. *"Ouch!"*

Tenel Ka looked perplexed, and Lowie groaned, but Sirra endeared herself forever to Jacen by chuffing uproariously at the joke. Then, after only a moment, Sirra sent her holographic fighter ahead of his with redoubled effort.

Little green lances of laser fire shot toward him, but he managed to roll his Y-wing and avoided getting himself blasted. Another Imperial ship clung to his tail, scoring hits and causing increasing damage as it came inexorably closer. Suddenly the pesky TIE fighter erupted in a tiny puff of an explosion with spangles of computer-imaged debris as Tenel Ka brought her Y-wing fighter to the rescue.

"It appeared that you needed some help, Jacen," she said.

"I did—thanks." He and Tenel Ka flew side by side as they followed close behind the streaking X-wings piloted by Lowie and Sirra. Their target approached, a small thermal exhaust port just waiting for them to drop a proton torpedo inside so they could blow up the horrendous superweapon Grand Moff Tarkin had built and—

The comm system chimed with a high-priority signal. Sirra reached out to pause the game, freezing the fightercraft images in position over the grid. Lowie hurried to receive the message, already blinking his golden eyes at the sudden emergency announcement that appeared on his screen.

Jacen and Tenel Ka went to look as Lowie

bellowed in alarm. "Master Lowbacca, what is it? Let me see," Em Teedee said. "How can you expect me to translate if you won't let me read the text?"

Lowie punched a button so that Jacen and Tenel Ka could see the message. The comm system translated the words on the screen back into Basic.

"Just a fragment," Jacen said, his blood growing cold. "Something interrupted the transmission."

"It appears serious," Tenel Ka said.

Jacen read, "Emergency . . . injured at computer fabrication facility . . . need your help . . . please come right away. We—" He frowned, feeling his heart start to pound. "But who sent it? Who could it be from?"

"It was sent specifically here, to this house," Tenel Ka said. "Someone must have wished to contact us directly."

"But only Jaina and Chewie know we're here," he said, "and they went off to one of the repair docks to work on the *Shadow Chaser*, not to the computer fabrication facility."

"Perhaps they changed their plans," Tenel Ka said.

Sirra yowled, and Lowie added his own roar. "Oh my," Em Teedee said, "Master Lowbacca and Mistress Sirra's parents are at the facility."

"We cannot ignore this problem," Tenel Ka said. "We must go now and confront it. This is a fact."

"You're right about that," Jacen said.

Lowie punched some buttons on the comm system controls a few times, then pounded the apparatus in frustration. "Master Lowbacca says he is unable to reply to the message," the translating droid said. "Something appears to be wrong with communications at the facility itself. They've been completely cut off from outside transmissions."

Lowie roared for his sister to summon the fastest bantha mount in the area, while he, Jacen, and Tenel Ka fastened lightsabers to their belts, ready for the worst. The four of them rushed out the door of the tree dwelling.

A shaggy bantha lumbered to their platform in response to Sirra's frantic call. The Sullustan crouching on the beast's wide neck appeared deeply weary, ready to go off shift— but when the two young Wookiees bared their teeth and roared that this was an emergency, the mousy alien perked up instantly. Jacen clambered aboard and reached down, offering his hand to help Tenel Ka up; she took the aid without complaint. Sirra and Lowie leaped onto the beast of burden's back, and the bantha plodded off.

"This thing can go faster," Jacen cried. "I saw them stampeding once on Tatooine."

Lowie barked an order and the Sullustan urged the creature to greater speed until its pounding feet vibrated the entire wooden walkway.

High in orbit over Kashyyyk, defensive satellites bristled with weapons, designed to target on invading enemy forces. But the satellites remained silent and motionless as a disguised shuttle, drifting in place, opened its hangar bay doors so that a squadron of TIE fighters could drop out.

Weapons powered up, the Imperial fighters ignited their twin ion engines with a loud roar and streaked toward the thick forest below, flying in tight formation. The general battle plan had already been input into their computers. The Imperials intended to strike swiftly, surgically, causing the greatest damage possible in as little time as necessary. They needed to grab their prize, then vanish into space.

Kashyyyk's defensive satellites picked up the enemy on their sensors and transmitted an urgent report, a call for action, to the control tower in the computer fabrication facility. The sensors continued to track the enemy's flight path, but they received no arming instructions or attack confirmation from the control tower. The planet remained silent. The satellites did not fire.

Although the satellites' weapons were inactive, the sensors continued to file data from the impending attack for future reference . . . if anyone on Kashyyyk survived the Imperial assault.

When the weary bantha finally arrived at the fabrication facility, Lowie, Sirra, Tenel Ka, and Jacen leaped off its back and rushed to the entrance.

The tall, spindly Tour Droid stood waiting. Seeing new visitors, it unplugged itself from a recharge port and assumed its security posture, since no guests were expected at the moment. "Halt!" it said.

"Where's the emergency? We've got to get inside," Jacen shouted.

"We are responding to the distress call," Tenel Ka said.

Lowie and Sirra both roared an explanation, believing that the Tour Droid might respond better to Wookiee than to Basic.

"No emergency has been reported," the Tour Droid said, its arms dangling from its shoulders like metal rods.

"There *must* be," Jacen said. "We received a high-priority transmission telling us to come immediately."

"Accessing," the Tour Droid said as it plugged one of its dowel-shaped fingers into a computer port. It paused a moment as a blur of characters streamed across the screen. "Are you certain you have the right coordinates? Could I offer you some promotional brochures?"

"Ah. Aha." Tenel Ka looked gravely toward Jacen. "Perhaps we have been tricked."

"Blaster bolts!" Jacen said. Hearing a roaring sound from high above, he pointed frantically to the sky. "It looks like there's *about* to be an emergency!"

Lowie tilted his head back and exposed his long fangs, howling in rage.

A wave of Imperial TIE fighters dropped out of the clouds, arrowing straight for the computer fabrication facility. Their weapons began blazing even before they arrived.

12

IT WAS COMFORTING to work with someone who loved machinery as much as she did,
Jaina thought. Apparently she and Chewbacca were the only ones around today.

Cool breezes crept in through the open bay
doors. The fresh air and the view out over the
ocean of leaves made her glad they kept the
hangar open. Constructed in a crown of trees
rising above the overall canopy level in an
outlying area beyond the Wookiee residential
district and the computer fabrication facility,
this hangar bay was used for major vehicle
repairs.

Aside from Jaina's and Chewie's clanking
and thunking noises as they tinkered, the
cavernous, wooden-walled bay remained relatively quiet and deserted. That was fine with
Jaina. She loved nothing more than relaxing
with a fine piece of equipment, making the
pieces fit together properly, fiddling with the
components.

And the *Shadow Chaser* was still state-of-the-art.

When Chewbacca bellowed a request up the boarding ramp, Jaina crawled out from under the cockpit control panel she was working on and hollered back. "Didn't get what you said, Chewie. *Which* tool are you looking for?"

A large hairy head appeared in the entryway and Chewbacca pointed to the tools he needed.

"Just about done here," Jaina said, hoisting the case up to where the Wookiee could reach. "I can finish up with my pocket multitool, so go ahead and take the rest of 'em." Chewie growled his thanks as Jaina crawled back under the console.

She completed her task, reattached the access panel, and trotted down the ramp, where she found Chewbacca cleaning lubricant off the lower armored hull. He rumbled a question.

"Did you ask me if I was hungry?" Jaina asked, struggling with the Wookiee language. She grinned. "Sure. Working on mode-variance inhibitors always gives me an appetite."

With another growl, Chewie spread his arms and shrugged.

"What are we waiting for?" Jaina interpreted with a chuckle. "Couldn't have said it better myself." Hearing a faint roar, like the sound of distant thunder, Jaina chuckled again. "Is that your stomach? You must really be hungry."

Chewbacca suddenly went still and cocked his head, as if listening. He squinted his blue eyes. The sound came again, this time punctuated by sharp thuds like blaster bolts hitting their targets, underscored by a low-pitched buzzing Jaina couldn't quite identify. "That's coming from outside," she said. "What could it possibly—"

Chewbacca held up his hand for silence. The Wookiee woofed and loped toward the hangar bay door, with Jaina hot on his heels. Outside, the treetops spread in a green and brown carpet well below the sheer edge of the hangar bay. Uprising branches held the hangar platform high above the remainder of the forest.

Peering out into the hazy sky, Jaina had no trouble identifying the overlapping sounds: explosions, blaster bolts, and a distinctive engine howl.

"TIE fighters! What would TIE fighters be doing here? And what are they firing at?" She looked at Chewbacca in alarm.

The Wookiee pointed in the direction the sounds had come from and barked an explanation: the computer fabrication facility.

Jaina groaned. "It has to be the Second Imperium! We never thought they'd strike here." Chewbacca roared in anger, and she needed no translation. "I know. We've got to get over there. Let's call for help—where's the closest comm unit?"

The Wookiee bounded to the communications panel next to the open bay door, slapped the switch, and bellowed an alarm. Jaina whirled as a stuttering whine erupted behind them. "Now what?"

The sound came from the *Shadow Chaser* itself. Chewbacca and Jaina exchanged glances and sprinted toward the sleek ship they had been repairing. Through the viewport, inside the cockpit, Jaina could see a petite woman with wavy bronze hair clad in polished lizard hide—a Nightsister.

"How did she get in there?" Jaina cried. "Hey, she's trying to steal the ship!"

The *Shadow Chaser*'s engines filled the hangar bay with a sound like millions of swarming insects. The whine stopped, started, then stopped again with a cough. The engines wouldn't fire. In the cockpit, the face of the

Nightsister twisted into a scowl. Her creamy brown skin mottled with rage.

Jaina looked up with equal anger. "We've got to stop her."

Chewbacca dove under the belly of the ship, barking reassurance.

"You're sure it won't start?" Jaina said. "How do you know?"

His head inside the still-open engine access hatch, Chewbacca grunted and nudged a piece of equipment on the floor with his foot. Jaina recognized the primary initiator module that the Wookiee had pulled for repairs.

The *Shadow Chaser* would never start—much less fly—without it.

The annoying whine came from the engines again, and Chewbacca yelped. There was a sharp thunk, and the noise stopped as a shower of sparks sprayed from the engine hatch. The Wookiee ducked back out.

Then Jaina heard the low hum of an extending entry ramp. But before they could rush aboard to apprehend the would-be thief, the Nightsister herself sprang out onto the hangar bay floor and faced them. Jaina thought there was something familiar about the set of the woman's face, the icy beauty and cold anger.

Chewbacca bellowed a challenge, but the

petite warrior rounded on the Wookiee, eyes blazing. "I came to reclaim my rightful property. You would be a fool to stand in my way. The *Shadow Chaser* is mine."

"Then you're that Nightsister—Garowyn," Jaina said. "Tenel Ka and Uncle Luke told me about you."

Garowyn shifted her glance to Jaina, her anger turning sour. "Why aren't you at the factory with the rest of your friends, Jedi brat?"

"Factory?" Jaina said in confusion. Why would her friends go there?

"No matter—it is too late to save them," Garowyn snarled, raising her arms overhead as if to hurl something, though her hands were empty. "It will all end here now—with me." She laughed. "You never had a chance."

Chewbacca bared his fangs and coiled his body, ready to lunge.

Suddenly, the meaning of Garowyn's words sank in, and Jaina cried, "We've got to help the others, Chewie! Forget about her." She ducked, hoping to make a run for the hangar bay door and the lift mechanism that would take them down to the main levels of the tree city.

"You're going nowhere!" Garowyn shouted.

One of several large wooden crates of engine components sailed through the air and knocked Chewbacca to his knees. He went down with a *woof* of pain and surprise.

Garowyn stood by the *Shadow Chaser*'s ramp, her hands on her scale-armored hips. With dark fire flickering behind her eyes, she used the Force to snatch other heavy objects from where they rested.

Jaina cried out as a similar crate flew directly at her head. She instinctively deflected it with a shove from the Force. Eerily, it reminded Jaina of the training sessions she had undergone while a prisoner at the Shadow Academy. Fear gripped her as the Nightsister tossed barrels, heavy bolts, mallets, metal sheeting, hydrospanners, and anything else she could fling, quickly and without moving a muscle, at her two captives.

Chewbacca tried to scramble for shelter behind a half-dismantled skyhopper, but Garowyn sent more sharp and hard objects flying after him.

While doing her best to deflect the flying objects from herself and Chewbacca, Jaina huddled behind one of the fallen crates and concentrated. Even in the midst of her own danger, she felt an urgency about reaching Jacen, Tenel Ka, Lowie, and Sirra.

Unfiltered lubricant oozed out of a broken

container, making an acrid-smelling puddle on the floor. Jaina was frustrated that she only had time to *react*. She was too busy defending herself to formulate any plan.

Though Chewbacca had no Jedi defenses, he also had no intention of remaining a stationary target. Jaina saw him slip away from the skyhopper's fuselage and lift a crate with his strong, hairy arms. With a powerful heave, he sent the crate smashing into an incoming pail of lubricant tossed by the Nightsister. As iridescent liquid sprayed into the air and splashed to the floor plates all around Jaina and Garowyn, Chewie scooped up his discarded toolkit and, with a mighty bound, leaped onto the hull of the *Shadow Chaser*.

"Tell me what you've done to my ship," Garowyn shrieked, now directing the barrage of objects at Jaina. "How can I fix it?"

The crate Jaina was crouched behind finally splintered under the attack, spilling hundreds of rattling, loose cyberfuses in every direction. Jaina scrambled to find other cover.

Panting, she dodged some of the thrown objects and deflected others with her skills. Perspiration streamed from her forehead and into her eyes, making it difficult to concentrate. "Damaged in an ion storm," she gasped, wiping an arm across her eyes. "You'll never be able to fly it."

"In that case, you're worthless to me," Garowyn sneered. "I'll take care of you immediately." Even as the Nightsister stretched out her hands, her fingers crackling with blue fire, Jaina cast about for a way to distract her.

From out of nowhere an impedance tester sailed toward Garowyn, followed by a hydrospanner and a barrage of rivets and heavy clamp-bolts. Chewbacca did not need the Force to hurl heavy objects.

Now it was the Nightsister's turn to dodge and deflect. Garowyn directed her attention to the Wookiee, and with a muttered oath sent a bolt of blue fire sizzling up at him. Chewbacca yowled and ducked, tumbling back over the opposite side of the sleek ship.

The distraction was brief, but it was long enough for Jaina. Reaching out with the Force, closing her eyes in concentration, Jaina gave the Nightsister's body a powerful shove.

Caught completely off guard, Garowyn slipped in the lubricant that coated the floor around her. With another forceful shove, Jaina sent her sliding toward the yawning hangar bay entrance.

"Give it up, Garowyn," Jaina said, her voice harsh with exertion. "You'll never get the *Shadow Chaser.*"

"You haven't seen the last of me yet," the Nightsister yelled.

Then, to Jaina's amazement, instead of trying to stop the momentum of her slide toward the gaping outer door, Garowyn gave herself an invisible shove in the same direction. Chewbacca scrambled after the woman, but the floor was too slippery for him to overtake her.

As she reached the entrance, Garowyn flung out one arm to grasp a vertical railing that ran along the edge of the doorway. Without slowing, she used her momentum to swing herself out and around in a tight half circle to land on the verandah that ran along the side of the hangar.

Wind whistled around the open door. Inside, the sounds of loose equipment clattered and clanked, and small components rattled out of broken crates. Jaina scrambled across the slippery floor plates, trying to reach the doorway through which Garowyn had escaped. Before she could reach the outside, Jaina heard a puttering, buzzing sound.

"Quick, Chewie," she cried, "she's got a speeder bike."

Jaina stumbled toward the entrance, slipping as she went. She grabbed on to a wall rail to prevent herself from pitching forward in a long drop to the canopy below.

Her heart sank when she saw the fleeing Nightsister on a speeder bike zip across the hanger bay opening, heading toward the computer fabrication facility, which Jaina knew was under attack from Imperial forces.

Moving with amazing speed, Chewbacca launched himself forward. To Jaina's horror, the Wookiee gave a ferocious howl and leaped straight out the door toward Garowyn's buzzing vehicle, with nothing beneath him but thin air—

—and grasped a pipe on the speeder bike with one strong, furry hand.

Still slipping, Jaina held the wall rail and watched Wookiee, Nightsister, and speeder bike spiral down toward the leafy sea. Jaina clung to the rail and reached out with one hand, but she was too far away to help Chewbacca.

As the speeder bike crashed on the treetops, Chewie quickly regained his balance.

The Nightsister, still covered with slimy lubricant, dismounted and scrambled for purchase on one of the narrow branches. Chewie swung himself to the thicker branch beneath her and shook the limb on which she stood, growling a challenge.

A harsh laugh escaped Garowyn's lips, and a triumphant look lit her face. Jaina could hear her voice even at this distance. "So you wish to die?" The Nightsister stretched out a hand that crackled with discharges of blue electricity. "You deserve it for what you've done to my ship."

Chewbacca, though defenseless in the face of her discharge of dark power, snarled at her.

In desperation Jaina tried the only trick that sprang to mind. Letting her eyes fall half closed, Jaina sent a rippling furrow through the leaves behind Garowyn. This time the invisible plow made a loud, rustling sound, like a stampede.

The Nightsister whirled to defend against the supposed attack on her from behind. Flinging up an arm to ward off her unseen enemy, Garowyn lost her footing on the narrow branch. She fell backward.

Jaina gasped as she heard Garowyn's head strike a lower tree branch with a solid *thud*.

Without another sound, the Nightsister's compact body tumbled like a shooting star, through the sharp and clinging branches into the depths of the jungle far, far below.

13

THE SCREAMING SOUNDS of TIE fighters ripping through the atmosphere sent a chill of primal terror down Jacen's spine. He knew the howl was only exhaust from the powerful engines, but he felt certain the Imperial ship designers must have delighted in the hellish noise.

In the bustling fabrication facility, a cacophony of alarms rang out from platform loudspeakers. Growling, barking announcements hammered through the air. Wookiee workers ran in all directions, activating security systems or evacuating the area.

TIE bombers streaked low over the treetops, dropping proton explosives that set the dense network of branches aflame. Dark gray smoke billowed from burning leaves.

"We must help defend against this threat," Tenel Ka said, looking for some weapon substantial enough to use against the invading fighters. Her face wore an expression of stony determination.

Sirra and Lowie howled in rage at seeing the destruction of the tree dwellings. The spindly Tour Droid spun its boxy head around, despite its numerous optical sensors. "Do not panic. Have no fear," it said in its tinny voice. "This must be a drill. No attack has been scheduled for today."

At Lowie's waist, Em Teedee piped up in a scornful tone. "Why, you silly Tour Droid, switch on your optical sensors! Can't you see this is a crisis situation? Hmmmf!" The miniaturized droid muttered a deprecating comment about the questionable intelligence of public-relations models.

The Tour Droid continued to issue calming messages, though its thoughts were obviously scrambled. "Kashyyyk has numerous satellite defenses. No enemy ships can approach this facility. We have sophisticated defense mechanisms, including powerful perimeter guns. They should begin firing any moment now."

"Perimeter guns?" Tenel Ka said, her cool gray eyes flashing. "Where? Perhaps we can use them against these enemies."

Sirra roared, gesturing with her long hairy arm to show that she knew the way.

"A splendid idea," Em Teedee said. "I do hope we won't be blown to bits before we can implement Mistress Tenel Ka's plan. Oh my!"

"As my sister would say," Jacen said, "what are we waiting for?" He, Tenel Ka, and the two young Wookiees barged past the Tour Droid into the complex.

Sirra led them down an open-air corridor amid the din of explosions and laser blasts. They reached a network of pulley-driven vines, ropelike lifts that yanked them to a higher level. Sirra grabbed one vine, tucked her foot into a loop, and the rope sprang upward, drawing her toward the higher platforms. Lowie did the same. Jacen followed suit, looking down to watch Tenel Ka, who wrapped her arm around the vine and stepped into a loop with no problem whatsoever. Within seconds, they were all whisked to an upper platform at the outer perimeter of the complex.

Because of their quick reaction, the companions reached the defensive guns before most of the Wookiee defenders. Jacen saw unattended ion cannons with spherical power sources and needlelike barrels aimed toward the sky—but his eyes lit upon a pair of old-model quad-laser cannons, exactly like those in the *Millennium Falcon*'s gun wells.

"Hey, we can use those!" Jacen said. He

raced over to the nearest emplacement, checking the status panels. "They're powered up and ready to go." Tenel Ka gruffly agreed and stationed herself behind one of the other weapons.

The two Wookiees chattered to each other. Em Teedee called, "Master Jacen! Master Lowbacca and Mistress Sirrakuk have decided to use the computers to determine where the breakdown in the facility's defensive systems occurred. Perhaps they can prevent further Imperial fighters from getting through. Oh, I do hope they're successful."

"They'll do their best," Jacen said, grabbing the quad-laser's targeting controls. He sank down into the voluminous seat in front of the cannon, feeling the energy thrum through the firing sticks in his fingers. Since the widely spread controls had been designed for large Wookiee bodies, he adjusted the targeting circle.

Imperial fighters continued to howl overhead, launching strikes against the Wookiee residential districts, but leaving the central computer facilities relatively untouched . . . though thrown into complete chaos.

A glance to Jacen's left told him that Tenel Ka was in position. Gripping the firing stick with her right hand, she seemed already familiarized with the weapon's control systems. In seconds her eyes began to track the enemy fighters overhead.

Three tall Wookiees charged onto the defensive platform and took up positions at the ion cannons, glancing curiously at the two humans, confused by this unexpected assistance. But they didn't waste time asking for explanations. Instead, they fired powerful blasts from the ion cannons.

One of the crackling yellow-white shots caught a TIE fighter that soared through the edge of the blast. The Imperial control systems flickered out and the TIE fighter spun dead in the air, its engine silenced. Unable to regain control, the pilot crashed into the distant forest canopy with a dull, booming explosion.

Jacen used his targeting circles to lock onto a sluggish, fully loaded TIE bomber that arrowed toward the clustered residential structures. The bomber came in, picking up speed while preparing to drop its deadly explosives.

Jacen grasped the firing controls and gritted his teeth. "Come on . . . come on," he said. Finally, the target lock blinked as the TIE bomber settled directly in the crosshairs.

He squeezed both controls, launching sear-ing blazes of laser energy from all four can-nons. The beams targeted on the bomber just before it could drop its proton explosives. Instead of destroying the homes of hundreds of Wookiees, the bomber became a brilliant ball of fire and smoke. The belch of detona-tions grew louder as the TIE fighter's own proton bombs fed into the eruption.

"Got one!" Jacen crowed.

Tenel Ka fired repeatedly until another pair of TIE fighters exploded in the air. "Two more," she said.

By now, additional Wookiee defenders had arrived to assume positions at the remaining guns. Jacen fired again and again, rotating his chair to aim at the rapidly moving tar-gets. He blasted another TIE fighter out of the sky.

"Just like our practice runs in the *Millen-nium Falcon*," he said. "Only this time, hit-ting the targets is a lot more important than winning a contest with my sister."

"This is a fact," Tenel Ka said.

Another wing of TIE fighters swooped down, and Jacen shot wildly. So many Imperial tar-gets, he thought, all of them bristling with lethal weaponry. . . . His quad-laser cannon spat beams of energy, but they all missed as the fighters spun evasive loops in the air.

"Oh, blaster bolts!" Jacen said.

Wookiees kept appearing, leaping off the vine pulley-lifts and rushing to their positions, although now there were more defenders than guns. Lowie and Sirra hurried over to Jacen and Tenel Ka, speaking loudly. Their grunts and growls overlapped, so that Em Teedee had difficulty translating both.

"One at a time, please!" the little droid said. "All right, I believe I understand the basics of what you're saying. Master Lowbacca and Mistress Sirrakuk have determined that a single-point defensive failure occurred in the traffic control tower for this facility. Somehow, all of the central command systems have been compromised. It appears that the attack is being guided from there."

Lowie roared a suggestion. "Oh dear," Em Teedee said. "Master Lowbacca suggests we would be well advised to go to the heart of the problem and leave these well-trained Wookiee gunners to continue the fight here. While I agree that it might be safer to move inside—I am skeptical about the wisdom of rushing into greater danger."

"Good idea, Lowie," Jacen said, ignoring Em Teedee's warnings. He fired the quad-laser one more time, almost offhandedly, and was astonished to see his quick shot destroy the side panel of another TIE fighter, which spun out of control and crashed to the tree-tops. "Hey, got another one," he said.

Barricaded in the traffic control tower, Zekk listened to outraged Wookiees pounding against the sealed door. A sizzling, melting sound worked its way into the background din as the Wookiees used high-intensity laser torches to slice through the armored metal. Their own well-constructed defenses worked against them, since they had intended Kashyyyk's command center to be impregnable. Slowly but surely, though, the Wookiees made headway, slicing through the door one centimeter at a time.

Using the security monitors, Zekk watched the hairy creatures out in the hall. With bestial rage one of them picked up a metal pipe and hammered at the door—to no effect, of course, because of the thick plating, but the Wookiee seemed satisfied just to be able to vent his fury.

Tamith Kai crossed her arms over her reptile-armored chest. "The noise level out there is most annoying," she said, then glared at the stormtrooper standing guard.

Her violet eyes flashed with a twisted idea. "Why don't we trigger the locking mechanism and let the Wookiees stumble inside. We can easily take care of the whole lot before they recover from their surprise."

Vonnda Ra chuckled. "That would be amusing to watch."

Before Zekk could voice an indignant protest that *he* was in command of this mission, the stormtrooper activated the door controls. The panel suddenly slid aside, shocking the Wookiee engineers who had been working to gain access. They howled.

The stormtrooper used his blaster rifle to mow them down in a few seconds, every one of them. Even encased in white armor, the stormtrooper's body language showed his pleasure. He keyed in the sequence to slam the heavy door shut again, leaving the fallen Wookiees out in the corridor.

"At last, peace and quiet," Tamith Kai said.

Overhead, TIE fighters and bombers continued to attack, dodging bursts of weapon fire from the tree facility's perimeter defenses. The reinforced dome overhead showed the battle in the skies. Several contingents of stormtrooper reinforcements had already landed.

Vonnda Ra worked at one of the computer stations, scanning security images. A minute later, she gave a gasp of surprised triumph. "Ah, I believe I've found them," she said. "The vermin were firing the perimeter guns, but now they're in the corridors. They seem to be making their way . . . ah! They're making their way here. Delusions of grandeur. That could prove quite convenient."

"Who?" Zekk said.

Vonnda Ra raised her eyebrows. "Why, those Jedi brats, of course. Had you forgotten your other goal for this mission?"

Zekk thought of Jacen and Jaina and their friends. "No, I didn't forget," he said. But he didn't want to confront the twins here, not in front of the evil Tamith Kai. This should have been his own private battle, the consequences of the choices *he* had made. "We'll meet them on the way. Ambush them. Lock down their location."

"Simple enough," Vonnda Ra said.

Reinforcing his position of command, Zekk turned sharply and issued brisk orders. "Tamith Kai, you will remain here and continue organizing the mission. Our primary goal is to get those computer systems for the Second Imperium. You—" he nodded toward the stormtrooper "—will stay here as guard.

Vonnda Ra and I will take care of the young Jedi Knights."

Tamith Kai scowled at being ordered about, but Zekk rounded on her, his cape swirling. "Is that assignment beyond your capabilities, Tamith Kai?"

"Indeed not," she said. "Is yours? Just be certain you eliminate those brats."

When the stormtrooper unsealed the armored door again, Vonnda Ra followed Zekk, and they strode out into the corridor, stepping around motionless Wookiee engineers sprawled on the floor, heading toward a confrontation with Zekk's former friends.

Jacen rushed along, shoulder to shoulder with Lowie and Sirra. The interior corridors were full of smoke, debris, and noise. Glowpanels in the ceilings flickered off and on with energy fluctuations from the attack.

Jacen and Lowie drew their shimmering lightsabers and held them ready. Tenel Ka picked up a loose metal rod, a piece of destroyed pipe that had fallen from an overhead assembly, and loped along behind them, guarding the rear. She held the rod like a spear, as if hoping to find some enemy target.

Lowie and Sirra turned the corner in the corridor, and Jacen thought he recognized the route they had taken to the monolithic control tower during their visit with the Tour Droid. Suddenly, Lowie gave a surprised roar; Sirra bellowed in alarm. Tenel Ka brandished her long metal rod.

"Hey, it's Zekk!" Jacen shouted, skidding to a stop.

There in the corridor, as if waiting for them, stood the dark-haired scamp who for years had been a friend to Jacen and Jaina . . . who had taken them on excursions through Coruscant's abandoned building levels and dim alleys. Now the once-scruffy boy wore expensive leather armor and a crimson-lined black cape—and bore a scarlet-bladed lightsaber. He looked ominous.

Tenel Ka saw Zekk, too, and held her metal staff at the ready. In a flash of memory, Jacen thought of the warrior girl's initial meeting with Zekk, back on Coruscant: when the young man had dropped down from above to surprise them, Tenel Ka had whipped out her fibercord with blurring speed and lassoed him before he could jump out of the way.

Now, though, Tenel Ka had only one hand, and she did not choose to drop her long steel rod to grab for her rope, or her lightsaber.

For a moment Zekk's face seemed to open.

His eyes grew round and uncertain. "Jacen," he said, "I—"

Tenel Ka glared at the Nightsister and spoke in a low, threatening voice, "I have your name, Vonnda Ra. I saw you try to lure others from the Singing Mountain Clan on Dathomir. In your encampment at the Great Canyon you chose me as a trainee for the Shadow Academy, but instead we rescued my friends—and defeated you utterly. We'll defeat you again."

The muscular Nightsister held up her claw-like hands. "Not this time, Jedi brats!" she said. "I shall enjoy destroying you."

Jacen felt her dark power crackle through the air, and he held his lightsaber high in defense. Fire-blue lightning bolts danced at Vonnda Ra's fingertips, burning through her body and sizzling behind her eyes.

She flicked her wrists to hurl her dark lightning at them—but Zekk shouldered the Nightsister to one side. The bolts of evil force flared past them like shadowy flames and scorched the wall plates.

Vonnda Ra glared at Zekk, but he snapped, "They are mine to deal with! *I* am in command here."

With a thundering sound of booted feet, a contingent of Imperial fighters charged down the corridor. Jacen looked up in alarm. Reinforcements had arrived—far more than he could hope to fight with his lightsaber, even with the help of Lowbacca, Sirra, and Tenel Ka.

Stormtroopers must have landed on the upper platforms, Jacen surmised. The Second Imperium apparently wanted something here at the fabrication facility. Judging from the alarms and explosions, the Imperials had already overrun most of the platforms.

Zekk stood waiting to battle the Jedi trainees, as if gathering up his courage and his anger, while the rebuffed Nightsister seethed with dark fury. The stormtroopers drew their weapons.

Jacen knew with sudden certainty that they could never win a face-to-face fight here. Tenel Ka pushed herself one step forward, brandishing her metal rod. "We must turn back," she said, darting a look at him over her shoulder.

"Good idea," Jacen said, casting a glance behind him.

"You, girl, are a traitor to Dathomir!" Vonnda Ra spat, just as Tenel Ka hurled the long pipe in her direction. The rod struck the Nightsister, knocking her sideways. Stormtroopers clattered toward them as Lowie and

Sirra turned to charge back down the corridor.

"After them!" Zekk called, gesturing with one black-gloved hand.

The stormtroopers thundered in pursuit. Vonnda Ra cast the pipe aside. Patches of it were bent and red-hot where fire from within her fingers had super-heated the metal.

Sirra yelled something to her brother as they sprinted down the corridor, with Jacen and Tenel Ka right behind them. "Access hatch?" Em Teedee translated. "Escape? Yes, that sounds like an excellent idea. By all means, let us escape."

At an intersection of corridors, Sirra stopped beside a clearly marked floor panel. Reaching her long fingers down, she hooked the tiny ring-handles. With her powerful muscles, she hauled upward, pulling the heavy hatch free to reveal a trapdoor. She growled and gestured.

Without hesitation Lowie leaped into the hole, catching a strong vine that hung underneath. The tinny voice of the translating droid wailed, "But this leads to the underlevels of the forest! Master Lowbacca, we *can't* go down here. It's far too dangerous!"

Lowie merely grumbled and continued his descent. Tenel Ka followed next, hopping lightly over the edge, wrapping her muscular legs around a vine. Grasping it with her hand, she lowered herself into the darkness.

Jacen turned around just in time to see Zekk and Vonnda Ra rushing toward them, flanked by stormtroopers. "Down into the underworld, huh?" Jacen said, glancing at Sirrakuk. "Looks like you'll get an early chance to complete that risky adventure of yours."

Sirra growled her agreement. With that, both of them plunged over the lip of the trapdoor and descended into the murky, leafy depths below.

Scrambling downward into the tangled foliage, Jacen looked up through the dense branches to see the silhouetted figures of Zekk and Vonnda Ra conferring at the edge of the glowing patch of light. Jacen could hear their voices faintly as he fled deeper into the thick forest.

"We'll have to follow them," Zekk said.

"You should have allowed me to destroy them when I had the chance," the Nightsister snapped. "Now they will cause difficulties."

Zekk answered sharply. "*I* am in charge here. We'll do things my way." He turned and shouted to the stormtroopers. "Down into the forests. All of you."

Zekk, Vonnda Ra, and the stormtroopers plunged after their prey into the underworld of Kashyyyk.

14

BRAKISS PACED THE corridors of the Shadow Academy, like an inspector general ensuring that his troops were prepared for imminent combat. He glided along with silent footsteps. His robes whispered around him.

The Master of the Shadow Academy looked too clean, too handsome to be an ominous threat. And although command of the new Dark Jedi rested firmly in his hands, his mind was instead focused on resolving his own doubts.

Brakiss allowed a flicker of anger—*anger,* the heart of dark side power—to flash through him. His right fist clenched . . . then he dismissed the emotion. He must not lose control, he told himself, for therein lay a greater weakness. Now he must be strong.

Through his own work, he had created the armored space station as a Dark Jedi training center. He had done it all for the glory of his Great Leader, to help bring about the Second Imperium and restore the galaxy to order and firm paternal control. He had done so much work, risked so many things. . . .

And now the Emperor had snubbed him.

Since the secret Imperial transport had arrived at the Shadow Academy and the four scarlet-cloaked Imperial guards had taken Palpatine's sealed isolation chamber off to a restricted section, Brakiss had neither seen nor spoken to the Emperor, despite his many requests for an audience. He had been so honored to learn that the Great Leader would visit. . . .

But now Palpatine's presence threw all of his thoughts and plans into turmoil.

Brakiss glided along the curved corridors. The lights had been dimmed for the sleep cycle; most of the Dark Jedi students had sealed themselves inside their quarters for the evening. A small shift of stormtroopers continued their patrol duties.

Qorl had been successful in training new military recruits from the Lost Ones gang on Coruscant. The TIE pilot had paid particular attention to the burly Norys, who had a knack for Imperial enforcement techniques—though the insolence Norys showed gave Brakiss cause for concern. Still, only rarely did stormtrooper trainees show such . . . enthusiasm.

As Brakiss drifted along the quiet corridors, he fleetingly wished he were wearing stormtrooper armor himself, so that his footsteps could make resounding, forceful clangs. But unfortunately, such a demonstration of pique would have been deemed unworthy of a Jedi superior.

Brakiss was a powerful man—or so he had thought, until the Emperor's entourage arrived. The red guards seemed to consider him the lowliest of servants. This was an unfair dismissal of all he had accomplished, he told himself. Perhaps the Emperor truly was ill; perhaps the Second Imperium was in greater danger than Brakiss had feared. He decided it would be best to speak directly to Palpatine, to see for himself.

He had been patient. He had been helpful. He had accommodated every whim passed along by the faceless Imperial guards—but now Brakiss needed answers.

Brakiss took a deep breath to center himself, to focus his thoughts to a razor edge of calm resolve. Propelled by his growing confidence, he turned about and made his way

toward the isolated chambers of the Emperor
and his followers.

Brakiss would not be turned away this
time.

The section reserved for the Emperor's
group seemed even dimmer than the rest of
the Shadow Academy. The light had been
polarized somehow, so that it contained a
reddish tinge that made it difficult to see.
The ambient temperature felt colder.

Two red guards stood posted at the intersection of the corridor. They towered over
Brakiss as he approached, the folds of their
scarlet robes gleaming in the reddish light as
if they had been oiled. The guards carried
force pikes, ominous-looking weapons that
might simply be ornamental . . . but Brakiss
did not want to test that theory.

"No intruders are allowed," one of the red
guards said.

Brakiss stopped short. "I believe you are
ill-informed. I am Brakiss, Master of the
Shadow Academy."

"We are aware of your identity. No intruders beyond this point."

"I am not an intruder. This is my own
station," he said, taking another bold step

forward and trying to impart power to his words.

One of the guards shifted his force pike. "This station belongs to the *Emperor*. He holds the right to claim ownership of everything he considers valuable to his Second Imperium."

Following that thread of argument would do him no good, Brakiss decided. "I must speak with the Emperor," he said.

"That is impossible," the guard answered.

"Nothing is impossible," Brakiss countered.

"The Emperor sees no one."

"Then let me speak to him over the comm. I'm certain he will wish to see me once he and I have had a brief discussion."

"The Emperor has no desire for 'a brief discussion'—with you or anyone else."

Brakiss placed his hands on his hips. "And when did the Emperor delegate the authority to speak for him"—he spoke the words scornfully—"to his mere *guards*? By what right did you become his mouthpiece? I do not recognize your authority, *guard*. How do I know you're not holding him hostage? How do I know that he isn't ill or drugged?"

He crossed his arms over his robed chest. "I accept orders only from the Emperor. Now let me speak to him immediately, or I shall call forth all of my troops on this station and arrest you for mutiny against the Second Imperium."

The two red guards stood motionless. "It is unwise to threaten us," they said in unison.

Brakiss didn't back down. "It is unwise to ignore me," he replied.

"Very well," one guard said, and turned to a comm station on the wall. He pushed a button and, though Brakiss heard no words from beneath the armored helmet, the Emperor's voice instantly slid through the speakers, like sounds made of snakes.

"Brakiss, this is your Emperor. Your insolence annoys me."

"I merely wish to speak with you, my lord," he said, forcing his voice to remain steady. "You have not addressed the Shadow Academy or me since your arrival here. I am concerned for your personal well-being."

"Brakiss, you forget your place. You can do nothing to protect me that I cannot do myself—with ten times the power."

Brakiss felt his anger dwindling, but he clutched his pride for one last moment. "I have not forgotten my place, my lord. My place is as the Master of the Shadow Academy, to create an army of Dark Jedi for you and your Second Imperium. My place is *at your side*—not cast out and ignored like an insignificant bureaucrat."

Palpatine seemed to pause before snapping a reply through the speaker. "Do not forget, Brakiss, that when this station was constructed I saw to it that explosives were planted throughout the superstructure to ensure your obedience. I can destroy this Academy on a whim. Don't tempt me."

"I wouldn't dream of it, my lord," Brakiss said, feeling his anxiety grow. "But if I am to be part of your plans of conquest, I must be consulted. I must be permitted to give my input, because I alone can provide the valuable fighters you require to defeat the Rebels and their upstart new Jedi Knights."

The Emperor snapped, "You will learn of my plans when I wish you to learn of them! I require no advice from you or from any other. Perhaps you need to be reminded that you are merely an expendable servant. Do not demand to see me again. I will emerge from my quarters when it suits me."

With a click like the sound of a breaking bone, the comm unit switched off. Brakiss felt worse than ever. More insignificant, more confused.

The red Imperial guards stood firmly in

their positions, holding their force pikes upright. "You will depart now," one of them said.

Without replying, Brakiss spun on his heel and marched in silence down the hollow, echoing corridors of his Shadow Academy.

15

TOO STUNNED AT first to move, Jaina hung on to the edge of the hangar bay doors on the platform high above the rest of the treetops. She stared down in unwilling fascination at the spot where Garowyn had fallen through the branches. Replaying the scene in her mind, still not quite able to believe what had happened, she saw the Nightsister falling . . . *falling*.

By the time Jaina managed to tear her gaze away, Chewbacca had retrieved the speeder bike and buzzed back up toward her. With an urgent sound in his voice, he pointed to the explosions and flickers of laser cannon fire in the distant fabrication facility. TIE fighters shot overhead, pummeling the residential areas with bright energy bolts.

Chewbacca gestured with a long hairy arm, pointing to the seat behind him on the speeder bike. Jaina gulped. Surely he didn't intend for *both* of them to ride that thing? The tiny vehicle was already wheezing and chugging under the Wookiee's considerable weight.

On the other hand, the two of them had walked to the hangar bay this morning, and they had no other vehicle to take them to the besieged fabrication facility—and they had to help. There was no time to call for a bantha. She hoped her brother and her friends were all right.

Chewbacca brought the speeder bike to an unsteady hover in front of the repair bay and motioned for her to get on. Jaina squelched her reservations and climbed on behind him. She found little room to sit, and her legs were still slick from spilled lubricant, so she threw her arms around Chewie's broad chest as far as they would go, threading her fingers through his thick fur to keep herself from sliding off.

With Jaina's added weight, the speeder bike sank. Chewbacca revved its engine, and they took off. Though their forward progress was faster than Jaina had expected, the vehicle continued to lose altitude until it barely skimmed over the bushy treetops. The engine sputtered. Jaina could feel the toes of her boots brushing against taller branches and sprigs of leaves. The wind in her hair blew the strands wildly in every direction.

Jaina yanked her foot up to avoid an up-thrust bough, and nearly capsized the little speeder. But Chewbacca felt the change in balance and managed to compensate by shifting his weight in the other direction. Jaina clung to his fur and gratefully maneuvered herself back upright.

"Can't we go any faster?" she shouted into his fur-covered ear. Her heart pounded, and the sweat of fear evaporated in the cold breeze of their wild flight. The Wookiee roared back at her, clearly understanding the danger their friends might be facing.

When they reached the fabrication facility, Jaina could hardly believe her eyes. Grayish white smoke curled up from half a dozen different windows and skylights in the factory. Splintered and charred wroshyr branches lay scattered about like the broken playthings of a spoiled giant. Imperial fighters still flew in formation in the skies, but they dwindled in the distance, heading back to orbit.

"Is the attack over already?" Jaina asked in disbelief. Chewbacca echoed her surprise.

The Wookiee had a hard time controlling the laboring speeder bike as they landed, and both he and Jaina tumbled off. Not bothering to check their bruises, they picked themselves up and rushed to the closest entryway, calling for Jacen, Lowie, Tenel Ka, and Sirra.

The scene inside the factory was utter chaos. Frantic Wookiees rushed about bellowing orders, extinguishing small fires, righting toppled machinery, and helping injured or trapped friends. The smell of charred wood and singed fur stabbed at Jaina's nostrils. Pale chemical smoke stung her eyes, but most of the fires were already contained, and a fresh breeze blew in through the open windows to clear the fumes.

Chewbacca roared in recognition as he rushed to his sister Kallabow—Lowie and Sirra's mother. She was bent over another injured worker, tending his wounds. With nimble hands Kallabow had shaved the fur from around a bleeding cut and covered it with a coagulant bandage.

Lowie's mother looked up, blinking dazed eyes set within whorls of auburn fur, and she and Chewbacca engaged in a rapid, barking interchange. Jaina caught only parts of the conversation, but learned enough to know that the devastating raid was indeed over. The Imperials had struck with lightning speed, causing enormous damage to the outlying facilities—but their main objective had apparently been to raid the equipment stockpiles and steal computer components and encryption devices.

Jaina was reminded of Qorl's previous raid on the New Republic supply cruiser *Adamant*, when he had commandeered an entire shipment of hyperdrive cores and turbolaser batteries. The Second Imperium was definitely making plans for an all-out war—and soon.

Jaina bent down next to Kallabow. "Have you seen Lowie and Sirra? My brother Jacen, or maybe Tenel Ka?"

Lowie's mother rattled off a series of woofs, growls, and barks in a worried tone. She spread her arms to indicate the surrounding pandemonium, then gripped Jaina's shoulder, asking her to track down her children. Another Wookiee wailed in pain farther down the corridor; still dazed, Kallabow blinked wearily and moved past Jaina to help the victim to his feet.

"We've got to find them," Jaina said, and Chewbacca nodded vigorously.

Chewie made his way deeper into the damaged facility, assisting wherever he could and barking out phrases that were incomprehensible to Jaina. Never one to stand around wringing her hands in an emergency, Jaina helped to bind up minor wounds and put out small fires. Occasionally, she used the Force to help muscular Wookiees heave aside smashed equipment. Every time she asked about her brother and her friends, however, she received only confused answers.

Moment by moment, the cacophony around Jaina increased with a confusing mix of Wookiee yowls, barks, and growls. Oh, how she wished that Em Teedee were here to interpret all the nuances. Her head spun with confusion and disorientation, and she was relieved to see Chewbacca motion her over to help him tend a wounded engineer. Chewie greeted her with animated gestures and an excited bark.

"What did you find?" Jaina asked, biting her lower lip.

The injured engineer spoke, her voice just above a wheezing purr. Still unable to understand, Jaina turned to Chewbacca for an interpretation. The irony of the situation might have struck her as funny had the circumstances not been so serious.

Chewie explained slowly enough that Jaina could follow. The engineer had seen the two young Wookiees and two human visitors run down the corridor behind her. Not long afterward, she had noted some of the Imperial attackers in the same corridor—storm-troopers and humans in dark capes.

"Any way out in that direction?" Jaina asked hopefully. "Is it possible they escaped?"

The engineer shook her head. No exits, only maintenance trapdoors that opened to the dense and dangerous forests below.

Trapdoors.

Chewie finished binding the engineer's wounds, thanked her, and hurried off down the corridor she had indicated. Jaina skidded to a stop at the edge of a gaping hole blasted in the floor, where an access hatch had been ripped from its hinges. Chewbacca had to pull Jaina back physically to keep her from toppling over the brink. He growled, sniffing around the burned metal edges.

Jaina nodded. "Yeah, looks like the work of stormtroopers. They must've thought the trapdoors needed to be wider and did a little remodeling." She blew out a long, slow breath, trying to calm herself. "Lowie told us how dangerous it is down there. But I guess it didn't stop *them*."

Chewie opened an emergency locker on the wall. He yanked out two knapsacks filled with supplies and tossed one to Jaina. Then, with a barely audible growl, he pointed down at the hole in the floor.

"You're right, of course," Jaina said. "What are we waiting for?" She peered down into the inky darkness below.

"Your jungle," she said at last. "I guess you'd better lead."

16

DEEP INSIDE HIS hairy chest, Lowbacca felt his heart contract with primal fear. He had known since childhood the dangers of descending into the perilous, untamed forests of Kashyyyk. The darkened depths often proved deadly even to those who entered fully armed and trained.

Nobody went to the underlevels willingly . . . but now, with Zekk and Vonnda Ra and the stormtroopers pursuing them, Lowie knew the primeval forest was their only chance.

The last time he had ventured beneath the secure treetop cities had been to search out glossy fibers from the syren plant, from which he wove his prized belt. He had thought himself so brave to accomplish the task alone.

Sirra's friend Raaba had also gone by herself—because Lowie had. Despite her skills and courage, though, the dark-furred

Wookiee female had never returned. But Lowie was not alone this time. He and his friends could fight together against whatever dangers the forest held.

Above and behind him, he heard the crashing of boots and the snapping of twigs as armored Imperials followed them, shining brilliant glowbeams into the dank, forevernight levels, startling exotic creatures that had never seen the light of day. A few random shots rang out as stormtroopers blasted forest animals. Burned leaves smoldered, then went out in a gasp of thick smoke.

Lowie and Sirra did their best to lead Jacen and Tenel Ka, using their darkness-adapted Wookiee vision to find broad, sturdy branches along the trunks of the wroshyr trees. Panting with the desperate effort, Lowie wheezed encouragement. The friends pressed on blindly, with no specific destination, knowing only that they had to keep going if they were to lose their pursuers in the maze of the forest underworld.

Em Teedee's round, yellow optical sensors shed a bright glow into the murk, the most illumination they could risk. "Do be careful of those branches, Master Lowbacca," the droid said as a twig scratched his outer casing. "I wouldn't want to break loose and fall. That happened to me once already, if you'll recall, and it was a frightfully unpleasant experience."

Lowie groaned, remembering the misadventure on Yavin 4. Losing the translating droid had caused other problems as well, since no one at the Jedi academy had understood Lowie's warnings that Jacen and Jaina had been captured by the TIE pilot Qorl.

Behind them, lightning shot through the darkness and branches crackled as the stormtroopers opened fire again. Lowie instinctively ducked, and Sirra dropped to a lower branch without bothering to test it for sturdiness. Streaks blazed across the thickets, erupting in fire and choking smoke.

"Hey, look out!" Jacen cried.

Tenel Ka grabbed on to a branch with her hand and swung down to Sirra's level. "This way!" she said. "It is safe."

Lowie leaped after her, one arm around Jacen's waist, then sprinted across the moss-covered boughs. Farther from the warm sunlight, each forest level had a different ecosystem made up of matted platforms of interlaced vines, branches that grew together, accumulations of mulch in which other plants—fungi, lichens, squirming flowers—flourished. Thousands of insects, reptiles, birds, and rodents fled at the sound of the intruders.

Lowie chuffed for the others to follow him. Racing along on his flat feet, he wrinkled his black nose and sniffed the odor-congested air. His nostrils tingled with a tantalizing, terrifying scent—a scent he had smelled before. Something that had nearly cost him his life.

In the lambent glow from Em Teedee's optical sensors, Lowie saw the wide-open maw of a syren plant, its glossy-yellow petals atop the blood-red stalk looked like a gaping mouth waiting for a meal. The plant had somehow taken root in a crook between two intergrown branches, and fed upon denizens of this forest level. The sparkling fibers that formed a plume at the carnivorous flower's center shone temptingly bright, while a delicious scent lured unsuspecting victims.

Beside him, Sirra also sniffed the air and spotted the deadly plant. She growled in anticipation, her patchwork-shaved fur standing on end. But Lowie put a hand on her arm, shook his head, then gripped her arm firmly. He could tell his sister wanted to secure the precious syren fibers and prove her bravery as soon as possible.

Sirra groaned in disappointment, but she

clearly understood their priorities. Behind them, several levels up, the pursuing storm-troopers fired again, this time at some large creature crashing through the tree levels.

Far too dangerous. The Imperials were too close.

With a growl Sirra took the lead, and Lowie guided his friends behind her.

As she raced through the morass of branches, ducking her head to keep her red-gold braids from snagging on thorns or low-hanging limbs, Tenel Ka reveled in the calisthenics that pushed her body to its lim-its. But she would have preferred to do it without the threat of sudden death from the blaster of a stormtrooper.

Her reptilian armor covered only her torso, leaving her limbs unprotected from scratches and insect bites—but she did not allow such minor inconveniences to bother her.

As the companions ran deeper into the forest, Tenel Ka took care to maintain her balance and watched out for her friend Jacen. Though he was highly skilled in sensing strange life-forms, Jacen was not as physi-cally capable as she was. This was the chase. The hunt. Here *she* was in her element.

But at the moment Tenel Ka was not the stalker, but the prey.

Her reflexes were sharpened by her inability to see through the forest shadows. Her lightsaber could have lit the way, but she didn't dare ignite it for fear of drawing attention to their position. At the moment her focus had to be on simply running.

All around, she detected looming dangers that grew worse, more foreboding, as they leapt from one level to the next, descending into thicker and thicker primeval wilderness. Tenel Ka sensed that the two Wookiees felt the increasing threat; Lowie and Sirra moved more cautiously, supporting each other as they used their night vision to choose a path.

At a broad, open intersection of wide branches, the Wookiees paused, panting for breath. Jacen slumped beside Tenel Ka, utterly exhausted. They knew they couldn't stop for long.

During the brief rest, Tenel Ka remained standing. She turned in a slow circle, granite-gray eyes narrowed, sharply attentive for movement, for predators lurking in the surrounding trees. Her Jedi senses detected no dangerous animals, only a tingling underlying threat that grew more and more powerful.

Just then, a leathery plant tentacle wrapped quickly around Tenel Ka's waist and drew itself snug. Thin thorns dug into her flesh through her reptilian armor. She cried out—and suddenly the air around them came alive with whipping, writhing vines from above.

Both Wookiees howled and thrashed. Jacen yelped. The thorny vines yanked him into the air, legs kicking, hands flailing. In an instant Tenel Ka snatched out her lightsaber and— ignoring the threat of revealing their position to the stormtroopers—ignited the glowing turquoise blade. Her arm swept sideways, severing the vines that grasped her waist.

Jacen yelled again and managed to get his lightsaber out, too. Swinging it above his head, he slashed through the vicious plant stems with a sizzling, wet sound. The spicy smell of burned sap cascaded into the air.

Lowbacca roared and ignited his Jedi weapon, striking left and right with the molten bronze blade. Hungry tentacles snaked toward him, eager to pull the Wookiee upward to where the knotted cluster of vines came together in a cavernous opening that emitted a sound like rocks grinding together, a slavering gullet ready to smash them into digestible pieces.

Two of the vines caught Sirrakuk and wrapped themselves tightly around her arms. She bared her Wookiee fangs and, bunching her powerful muscles, ripped the vines free of the central stem with brute force. The plant seemed not to notice; it went on thrashing its tentacles, and its open gullet continued to mash and grind.

Within moments, three flashing lightsabers sliced away the clinging tentacles and left only twitching stumps at the end of the voracious vine creature.

"We've escaped!" Em Teedee said. "Oh, how wonderful!"

"This is a fact," Tenel Ka agreed. She examined the red welts and oozing scratches she had received during the battle, then looked up toward the next level of branches. "But our lightsabers have attracted the enemy."

The others turned to follow her gaze. On the branches above them, completely surrounding the group, stood a contingent of fully armed stormtroopers, their blasters pointed down at the young Jedi Knights.

Jacen shut off the emerald beam of his lightsaber and squatted on the branch, breathing hard as he surveyed the encircling stormtroopers. In other circumstances, he would have found the underworld of Kashyyyk fascinating, filled as it was with insects and trees, ferns, vines, flowers, lizards— a million new pets for him to inspect, then set free. He found many of the life-forms to be incomprehensible, unlike anything he had ever experienced. Even now, with stormtroopers like pale statues above, blasters at the ready and aimed at him, Jacen could sense the hidden creatures around them.

Near one of the stormtroopers who stood on a decaying branch, Jacen noticed that a broad patch of bark lay wet and damp, like a mottled tongue wrapped around the tree. It was slick, glistening, moving on a cellular level.

Two more dark figures joined the gathered stormtroopers. The ominous Nightsister Vonnda Ra, with her hard muscles, broad shoulders, and glittering black body armor, stood next to Zekk, his dark hair neatly tied back with a thong at the nape of his neck, his swirling scarlet-lined cape undamaged by leaves or twigs. The stormtroopers shone glowrods down on the scene.

"You are trapped, Jedi brats," Vonnda Ra said. "It could be amusing to watch you grovel for your lives—but I can assure you it would do you no good."

"We do not intend to grovel," Tenel Ka said, and the Nightsister glared at the young warrior girl from Dathomir.

Jacen focused his concentration on the wide, mysterious slick patch wrapped around the branch. It seemed like a river of damp leather, and as he concentrated, he felt a dim awareness, a rudimentary brain that was more a cluster of reflexes. But reflexes were all Jacen needed right now.

"I'm sorry it has come to this," Zekk said, "but I owe my allegiance to the Second Imperium now, and you are my sworn enemies. I can no longer deny it. That was my choice." Despite his words, the expression on Zekk's high-cheekboned face and the disturbed look in his green eyes showed Jacen how troubled he truly was.

One of the stormtroopers moved sideways to get a clearer shot at them.

Jacen watched. *Just a little more, just a little more . . .*

Perhaps he sent out the thought with the Force, because the stormtrooper did indeed take one more step. His heavy, booted foot planted itself squarely on the wide wet patch.

Without warning, the creature reacted.

A slithering flap of wet, slimy meat in the form of a monstrous sluglike beast raised itself from its sleeping position. The motion knocked the stormtrooper completely off the branch, and he tumbled screaming into the depths of the forest.

With a thick slurping sound the enormous slug creature reared up and up and *up*, thrashing from side to side, knocking two other stormtroopers from their positions. The Imperial soldiers were thrown into pandemonium, shouting and shooting.

Jacen did his best to send a thought to the thing, identifying the white-armored guards as the enemy and planting the idea that Jacen, the two Wookiees, and Tenel Ka were the slow-witted creature's friends.

Stormtroopers opened fire on the monster, but the blasters did little more than annoy it. Branches crashed and snapped. Energy bolts ricocheted around in the forest as the slug creature continued its reflexive attack.

Jacen stood transfixed, fascinated with the battle and the havoc the beast had already caused. Zekk and Vonnda Ra shouted conflicting orders.

The next thing Jacen knew, Tenel Ka slammed him aside. A blaster bolt sizzled past him as she wrapped a vine around her arm, grasped his waist, and dove to a lower branch. The two Wookiees were already ahead of them in their headlong flight.

Making quick use of the diversion, the young Jedi Knights continued down, *down*— dropping all the way to the bottom levels of the forest.

17

THE FOREST DARKNESS was so thick Jaina could practically taste it. She followed the agile Chewbacca more by sound than by any other sense, finding herself relying more and more on the Force to guide her hands and feet. The air was cooler here below the canopy. Jaina shivered, though she doubted it was entirely because of the drop in temperature.

With his sharp Wookiee vision, Chewie led the way without hesitation. He barked an occasional warning about a patch of slippery moss or a weak branch. Neither made any great attempt to keep quiet: their one concern was to catch up with their friends before it was too late.

Gradually Jaina's eyesight adjusted enough that she could make out the shadowy forms of tree trunks, black against deep gray. It wasn't much to go by, but it helped. Chewbacca made a snuffling sound and gave a low woof of triumph.

"They came this direction?" she asked.

He yipped an affirmative. Their smells were here. He detected four . . . no, *five* of them, as well as a faint smell of metal. Jaina decided he must be picking up on Em Teedee. Chewie growled low in his throat, muttering about other smells too: plasteel, burned branches, the thunderstorm-smell of ozone from blaster discharges.

Jaina's heart skipped a beat. "Definitely sounds like the Nightsisters brought stormtroopers down here with them."

Chewbacca increased his speed, following the fresh trail. Once Jaina misjudged the spacing and almost fell between a pair of tree branches that were farther apart than she'd thought. "Chewie, I can barely see," she said.

With a chuff of understanding, the Wookiee stopped briefly, rummaged through the emergency pack he had taken from the fabrication facility, and pulled out a small mesh jar. Jaina recognized a phosflea lure. He broke the seal.

Moments later, as if the glowing specks had materialized directly from the air, the lure's surface was covered with tiny phosphorescent insects. Chewbacca fastened the lure to a strap around Jaina's waist. The "light" now shed a pinkish glow directly in front of her that swirled like a comet's tail as she moved along.

Chewbacca pointed below Jaina to a freshly broken branch and the burned scoring from weapon fire. The others had come this way.

"You're right," Jaina said. "I can feel them, not too far ahead."

The Wookiee helped her across the broad gap and they resumed their descent. Jaina climbed after him, watching handholds and footholds more carefully now as the glowing phosfleas lit her way. A feeling of dread mounted more strongly within her as they descended to each deeper level. She could feel the weight of the overlying forest pressing down on them.

Unseen predators bounded across leafy limbs, pursuing their quarries; the shriek of victims fallen in the endless hunt echoed through the thick labyrinth of branches. Smaller creatures chirped, buzzed, and chittered. None of them sounded friendly to her.

Jaina knew that her friends were good fighters, but she knew, too, that even Lowie, the strongest of all of them, feared the jungles of Kashyyyk. That alone was cause for worry, but the young Jedi Knights and Sirra had more to fear than the deadly plants and animals that populated the lowest levels of the forest.

Jaina could feel that something was about

to happen. "No time to lose!" she urged. She picked up her pace. Chewbacca, sensing her urgency, did the same, barely taking time to rest his foot on one limb before bounding down to a lower branch.

In the distance Jaina heard a shout, a human voice that sounded loud and chilling, mixed with the wild noises. When she stopped to look in that direction, she saw flickers of light and heard the sizzle of blaster fire.

Just then, the rotting branch beneath her feet creaked and threatened to give way. In her haste, she had not bothered to check the branch before stepping on it. Chewbacca spun and reached out to pull her to safety on a thicker branch closer to the trunk. She scrambled for purchase.

But the whole side of the wroshyr tree must have been weakened by rot or disease, for at that moment the bough on which the large Wookiee stood gave way as well. Snapping and popping, the gnarled wood dropped out from beneath him.

Jaina watched, her mouth open in a silent scream, as Chewbacca plummeted, crashing into the darkness below.

18

EXHAUSTED, ZEKK STOOD with the light-saber still gripped in his sweaty hand. He found it hard to breathe the thick, cloying air of the underworld.

The smoking carcass of the dead slug beast, now sliced in pieces, lay draped across the overspreading branches. Burned slime bubbled with a noxious stench. Small fires crackled from stray blaster bolts that had ignited portions of the dense foliage. The surviving stormtroopers shouted to each other over helmet comlinks, completing their damage assessment.

Vonnda Ra stood trembling, jaw set, face drawn, as if the fury she had unleashed to fight the monster had drained her somehow. The new Nightsisters were supposedly proof against the physically damaging effects of the evil powers they invoked, but the tremendous battle Vonnda Ra and Zekk and the

stormtroopers had waged against the mind-
less slug had left her looking shriveled.

Zekk slumped against an upright tree trunk,
feeling the soft squish of blue moss mixed with
ichor from the slug creature.

Only four stormtroopers remained with
their party. The slug beast had crushed the
others or flung them into the unseen depths
below. Chunks of the dead thing sloughed off
the main branches, oozing down to where
rodents and scavengers rustled through the
darkness in a feeding frenzy.

Zekk heard a crash and a crackle of snapping twigs far behind them. Suddenly, with a
tingle through his own Force senses, he knew
that two others followed, attempting to catch
them—and he identified one of the pursuers.
In astonishment, he blinked his green eyes
into the forest shadows, reaching out with
the focused power of his senses.

"It's Jaina Solo," he said to Vonnda Ra.
"Behind us. She's coming this way." He planted
his black boots firmly on the branch. He
had to choose, but he could not. With all of
Brakiss's promises, he had never thought it
would be so difficult.

Ahead Jacen, Lowbacca, Sirra, and Tenel
Ka had succeeded in eluding Imperial pursuit so far—but Jaina, completely unaware,

was heading straight toward them. He would have to confront her himself.

"We must split up," Zekk said. "I will go back alone and stop Jaina. The rest of you, continue after these others."

"Yes." Peering ahead into the forest maze, Vonnda Ra seethed. "I'll make them pay for what they've done to us!"

With a gesture of her clawed hand, the Nightsister and the remaining stormtroopers set off after the young Jedi Knights.

Though Jacen fought to stay within sight of his companions, this deep level of the forest had become so dark he felt as if he were swimming through a pool of ink. Finally, surprisingly, the depths began to shimmer with wonder. He noticed the cold illumination of phosphorescent organisms, glowing insects, pulsing fungi and lichens that threw heatless chemical light into the smothering darkness.

All around him in the branches and leaves he could see spangles like starlight, as if— instead of being deep within a dense forest— he stood on a sprawling plain under a clear night sky. Jacen found it breathtaking, and nudged Tenel Ka's warm arm to get her attention. The immensity of it overwhelmed him. He had never thought he'd experience something so wonderful down here.

As he and Tenel Ka stared upward, wordlessly sharing the experience, an unexpected volley of blaster shots streaked across the jungle like fireworks. A sparking white-hot globe of fire blazed toward them like a meteor—the stormtroopers had shot a dazzling flareball that spewed light in all directions.

The flareball crashed into the crook of a nearby tree and lodged there like a tiny sun, sputtering as it burned hot and bright. The flare sharpened the shadows and washed the humid air with garish light, stripping away the cloaking darkness.

Jacen saw to his dismay that four stormtroopers were standing on a single wide branch and aiming their weapons at the exhausted Jedi trainees, though the brilliant flareball had dazzled their eyes as well.

Tenel Ka shoved Jacen away from her. "Hide!" she said, and dashed off into the thick branches. Jacen ducked just as a blaster bolt sheared off a steaming chunk of wood above his head.

A rustling noise through the branches told him that Lowie and Sirra had also fled. He heard somebody else, but he could see only the four stormtroopers. He wondered if it could be Zekk . . . and he wondered if his dark-haired former friend would show them any mercy.

"Oh, blaster bolts," he said as another shot tore through the air too close to him. "Hah—no kidding," he muttered to himself.

In the strobing light he could discern only brilliant colors dancing before his aching eyes. Then he glimpsed the flickering movement of a slender figure suddenly sprouting a bright turquoise blade—Tenel Ka with her lightsaber . . . and she was just beneath the four stormtroopers!

The Imperial troopers saw her, too. They shouted excitedly and took aim—but too late.

With a single stroke, Tenel Ka slashed through the bough that supported the stormtroopers. Her rancor-tooth lightsaber flared, and sparks spat off in all directions as her blade severed the centuries-old tree branch.

Tenel Ka dove out of the way. Wood cracked, vines snapped, and leaves were torn asunder under the enormous weight of the surprised Imperial soldiers. They fired randomly, shouting in panicked bursts through their comlink helmets as the branch fell away, spilling them into the forest floor below. The four stormtroopers toppled to their deaths, blaster rifles still firing.

Looking fiercely satisfied, Tenel Ka deactivated her lightsaber and clipped it to her belt. Jacen, standing within her view, gave the warrior girl a round of silent applause.

Farther down, in the shelter of a curved and stunted tree, Lowbacca crouched close to his sister Sirra as the thick branch bearing the four hapless stormtroopers plummeted past them through the darkness. With his dark-adapted Wookiee eyes, he could see Sirra sniffing the air, waiting.

Sirra seemed preoccupied with testing the air and studying her surroundings. Then Lowie caught a twinge of scent—the frightening, tingling aroma of a syren plant, a large one, farther below.

With a quiet groan, he searched the area with his golden eyes until he saw the monstrous carnivorous flower in the thick underbrush of the ground level, its glossy yellow petals spread wide, its blood-red central stalk giving off a tempting scent. Sirra maneuvered herself until she was above the dangerous plant, then sought a safe way to get down to it.

Suddenly, Vonnda Ra leaped out of nowhere and slammed into Lowie, her hands crackling with evil lightning force. Jolts of searing electricity coursed through Lowie, and his fur began to smoke even as he staggered backward with a bellowing roar, stunned and disoriented.

In a blur of claws and teeth, Sirra leaped into the fray, flashing her ferocious Wookiee fangs. Her strong arms pushed Vonnda Ra away from her brother. The Nightsister turned on Sirra and released a bolt of her sizzling evil power.

Sirra cried out in pain and stumbled, then regathered her strength, launching off with powerful leg muscles into a full-body tackle of Vonnda Ra. Together, they went over the edge of the slippery, moss-covered branch and out into open air, tumbling and slashing.

Lowie shook himself and leaped into motion, rushing toward his sister. He reached out and caught the falling Nightsister's black cape, but the tough, slick fabric slipped through his fingers.

Sirra and Vonnda Ra fell.

Lowie howled in despair as the two combatants careened directly toward the waiting jaws of the syren plant.

Struggling as they dropped, Sirra managed to get on top. With an impact heavy enough to knock the wind out of a gundark, they crashed onto the broad, deadly petals.

Vonnda Ra's back struck the soft sensitive tissues inside the syren plant's open maw first. Sirra instantly pushed herself up to her feet, but the huge petals squeezed together in a reflexive, hungry action.

Roaring, Lowie leaped off the high branch, frantic to do something. His attention fixed on the glossy petals as they contracted, folding around its two new victims. High above, Jacen and Tenel Ka yelled down to him.

Vonnda Ra squirmed as the plant's trap squeezed tighter. Lowie saw his sister's head disappear as the thick muscular petals swallowed her up. Only one arm with pattern-shaved fur extended from between the deadly flower's jaws.

Lowie reached the syren plant, then grasped the leathery petals with his clawed hands, pulling, straining. The roots of the plant squirmed, digging deeper into the forest loam.

Lowie didn't dare take out his lightsaber and slash the flower to pieces, because he knew that would kill his sister as surely as the plant would. He tugged, groaning, and the sealed petals peeled slightly apart. The syren plant made a gurgling, gasping sound. Sirra's hand still protruded from the opening, flexing and struggling, as if she were in great pain.

While Jacen grasped a vine and began to climb down, Tenel Ka dropped beside Lowie, one of her throwing knives in her hand. She stabbed at the leathery wall of the plant, but her knife could not penetrate the tough skin.

Then a burst of black lightning and static from within caused the plant to convulse. Its petals flapped open again, as if in a gasp of agony. Inside, Vonnda Ra struggled to her knees, teeth gritted together and eyes blazing with the Dark Force concentrated in her. Lowie took the opportunity to reach in and get a firm grasp on Sirra. He pulled.

Laboring for breath, the young Wookiee moved as rapidly as she could across the slippery, shifting petals. Tenel Ka grabbed for Sirra's outstretched arm, and pulled. The syren plant began to contract. Jacen gripped the edge of one waxy petal to slow its closing and murmured low, soothing words to the plant. Lowie braced himself and leaned back, dragging his sister away with all his strength. Her feet slipped free of the petals just as the syren plant clamped shut again—with Vonnda Ra still inside.

Its deceptively beautiful, fleshy yellow petals squeezed with viselike muscles, squashing its remaining prey. A few flashes of black lightning flickered from within the plant, and

Vonnda Ra gave one last, muffled cry. The lumpy form caught in the folds of the flower struggled once, twice, then subsided into stillness.

Lowie held Sirra, knowing she might be injured and might need help to get back up to the higher levels. He noted with anguish the burned patches on his sister's fur where Vonnda Ra's power had singed her—yet to his amazement Sirra seemed happy, even delighted. She let out a roar of greeting.

Her eyes sparkled as she lifted her other arm up so he could see what she was clasping as if it were the greatest treasure she had ever held. During her ordeal inside the syren plant, before it had opened long enough for her to escape, Sirrakuk had managed to grasp a handful of the gossamer fibers with her trapped hand and yank them free.

She held up the silken strands in triumph, and Lowie barked with proud laughter. He embraced his sister and pounded her good-naturedly on the back with enough force to crack stormtrooper armor.

19

MOVING TO A stronger branch and gripping the tree trunk to ensure her balance, Jaina leaned over, anxiously peering into the forest depths where Chewbacca had tumbled. "Chewie!" she shouted.

She heard a Wookiee howl of pain rise toward her from the murky shadows below. He was still alive—and conscious—though she knew he must be injured.

Adjusting her grip on the vine-draped trunk of the wroshyr tree, Jaina bent over and cast the pale, pink light of the swirling phosfleas into the leaves below. As she had suspected, the light did not penetrate far enough for her to locate her friend. "Chewie, I'm here," Jaina yelled, using the Force to amplify her call. "Can you move? Can you climb back up here?"

She heard a far-off rustling and crackling of branches, then a loud yelp. Chewbacca groaned in dismay and then roared something about a fractured leg.

194

His words doused Jaina's sense of relief like an icy torrent of rain on a candle flame. A wave of weakness spun behind her eyes. Jaina clung to the tree, pressing her face against its rough bark.

Kashyyyk's jungle was dangerous enough for a healthy human with a full-grown Wookiee guide, but Jaina had no idea how to get *herself* out of the jungle—much less herself and an injured friend whom she'd undoubtedly have to carry. And then how could she help her brother and the others?

Meanwhile, she realized, Chewbacca's injury might even draw predators hoping for an easy kill. . . .

The thought snapped Jaina out of her momentary weakness. She had to think; she had to help Chewie. She was in training to be a *Jedi Knight*—and this problem certainly couldn't be impossible to solve, she told herself. First things first. She had to get down to Chewbacca right away. She felt ashamed that she had wasted precious seconds with her panic.

"Chewie," she yelled again, "keep calling to me until I find you."

She would have to move quickly. She felt around for a sturdy vine, yanking one after another until she found a rough strand that would hold her weight. Pressing the toes of her boots against the tree trunk, Jaina lowered herself hand over hand, maneuvering around the splintered stumps of branches broken by the Wookiee's fall. "I'm coming," she said, as much to reassure herself as to comfort Chewie.

By the time she located the injured Wookiee, her feet ached, her palms burned, and every muscle in her body shook with weariness. She unstrapped the phosflea lamp from her waist and held it close to Chewbacca's body to get a better look at him. The fuzzy light swirled as she moved.

A quick examination of his injuries told Jaina that the news was grim. The minor scrapes, bruises, and cuts could be dealt with easily enough, but one leg was broken. Chewbacca would never be able to walk out of here.

Jaina knew she was not equal to the task of transporting a wounded Wookiee hundreds of meters up to the forest canopy, even if she used the Force. She had barely made it this far herself.

Besides that, her brother and the others still needed her help. Jaina didn't know what she could do for them.

She thought the problem over while she used a few of the meager emergency supplies from their packs to clean Chewie's wounds. He groaned and did his best to help her.

Clearly, Jaina had no choice but to abandon her search for the others. Jacen, Tenel Ka, and the two young Wookiees were still fleeing from the Imperials. Jaina was no tracker, and she had little chance of finding them down here.

But she and her twin brother had always shared an uncommonly close mental bond, just like the one their mother Leia shared with her twin Luke. Perhaps if she sent out a cry for help, Jacen might be able to find *her*.

Concentrating all of her mental effort, Jaina sent out a cry—*"Help me!"*—that rang through her mind like a mallet striking a cymbal.

Opening her eyes, Jaina checked the fracture in Chewbacca's leg again. The bone fragments had not torn through the skin, but the injury was still serious. Jaina raised her phosflea light high and looked about for any sturdy material she could use as a splint.

The pinkish glow fell on a pair of black boots. A familiar voice said, "Did you call for help?"

Jaina started and nearly fell off the branch. Growling, Chewbacca bared his fangs, though he could make no move to attack.

"Zekk—what are you doing here?" Trying to check her astonishment, Jaina stood and held the glowing light higher, but the leather-clad figure took a step backward, keeping his face partly in shadow.

"I had business here on Kashyyyk."

"*Imperial* business?" Jaina asked, and bit her lip as soon as she had said it. Her heart contracted painfully. "What's happened to you, Zekk? How could you stay with the Shadow Academy? I thought we were friends."

He ignored the question, and asked two of his own. "Why are *you* here, Jaina? Why couldn't you have stayed away? I don't want to hurt you."

Chewbacca voiced a snarl of warning at these words, though at the same time he hissed in pain from his injury.

"Then don't hurt me, Zekk," Jaina said reasonably. She took a step along the branch toward her former friend. "I'm no threat to you. I'm your friend. I *care* for you."

"Step back and stay out of my way," Zekk snapped. "It's already too late for the others."

Jaina flinched and shut her eyes, feeling the blood drain from her face. Could it be true? Had Zekk already killed Jacen, Lowie, Tenel Ka . . . even an innocent stranger like Sirra?

No, she decided at last, it couldn't be. She would have felt it. Her brother and her friends were still alive. They had to be. She couldn't believe that Zekk's heart had become so scorched and black that he could murder someone he had once called a friend.

In an effort to distract him, as she had done with Garowyn, Jaina tried her trick again. She used the Force to riffle the leaves in the branches surrounding him, as if a chill wind were blowing through the claustrophobic cage of the forest underlevels.

Zekk looked up, his green eyes bright even in the shadows. It took him only a moment to realize what she was doing. His pale lips curled in a smile, then he gestured with one hand. The wind picked up, the branches clacked together, and a storm of dislodged leaves and twigs whipped through the air with the force of a small tornado.

Jaina shut her eyes, shielding them and shrinking back from the whirlwind. Chewbacca yowled, but Zekk paid no attention to the Wookiee. "I'm not impressed with your tricks, Jaina," he said. "Don't play games with me."

Then, with a *whoosh*, a sizzling brightness stabbed through her eyelids. Jaina opened her eyes to see Zekk holding the weapon of a

Jedi, his face lit by its pulsating scarlet glow. "Don't go for your lightsaber, Jaina," he warned.

She shook her head. "I won't raise a weapon against you, Zekk. And I don't believe you'd kill me either."

Zekk's face distorted with warring emotions. "Then stay away from the Jedi academy. If you ever get out of here, don't go back. The Second Imperium will soon target Yavin 4—and I will fight as a loyal warrior for my Emperor."

"Emperor? Zekk, you don't know what you're saying," Jaina pleaded.

"Stop treating me like I'm an ignorant street kid!" he snarled back. "You've always underestimated my abilities, denied me opportunities. But Lord Brakiss doesn't. He has shown me what I'm capable of." He tilted his head to look up into the dark nest of branches overhead, as if he could see the daylight far above.

"I've already sent a signal for a fast ship to pick me up. I believe our raid has been quite successful. Time for me to return to the Shadow Academy."

Zekk twitched his lightsaber from side to side as if shaking a finger in warning. "For the friendship we once had, I'll spare you this time, Jaina. But don't ever test my loyalties again."

With a harsh laugh, Zekk swept his light-saber upward, releasing a storm of leaves and twigs that showered down on Chewie and Jaina, knocking the phosflea light from her hand. Jaina ducked and covered her head. She couldn't see.

A moment later Zekk was gone, his hollow laughter ringing behind him as he left them in darkness.

20

LEFT ALONE AGAIN, Jaina shouted once more through the Force as the deep forest sounds grew thicker, more threatening around her. Predators, hidden in the leafy branches, cautiously approached, attracted by Chewbacca's muffled sounds of pain. They sensed helpless victims, easy prey.

"We need help!" she called. Her words quickly died to silence in the jungle gloom.

Then a blaze of rainbow light shattered the shadows: a flash of turquoise, a streak of emerald green, a slash of molten bronze. Lightsabers, like hot machetes, chopped the underbrush aside. Jacen, Lowie, and Tenel Ka pushed their way forward, with Sirrakuk following close behind, grinning so widely her fangs flashed in the vibrant light.

Chewbacca bellowed a greeting, and Lowie and Sirra clambered up to help their uncle.

"Hey, Jaina!" Jacen called. "Are you all right?"

She wiped grimy tear streaks from her cheeks, still shaken from the confrontation with her former friend. "I'll survive," she said, then drew a deep breath. "Zekk was here. He said the Second Imperium is going to wipe out the Jedi academy, and that he was going to fight along with them."

Lowie growled, looking up from tending Chewbacca. Tenel Ka stood rigidly, holding her rancor-tooth lightsaber high. "Not if we can help it," she said.

Jaina indicated the injured Wookiee. "We have to get Chewie up and out of here. I think his leg is broken—nothing a medical droid and a few hours in a bacta tank can't fix. But if we don't get back up to the treetops, we're all going to be somebody's lunch."

Sirra growled in defiance. Now that she had succeeded in her dangerous quest against the syren plant, Lowie's sister looked as if she could take on the whole jungle by herself.

As the two strong Wookiees carefully eased their uncle to a standing position, Jacen and Tenel Ka did what they could to help, using the Force and their hands. Jaina took the lead along with Sirra, blazing a trail with her lightsaber.

Together, the companions made their way back up to the light.

21

THE CAMOUFLAGED ASSAULT shuttle hovered in the void of space, waiting for confirmation, until the Shadow Academy shut down its cloaking shields. The ominous spined ring of the Imperial training station shimmered into view just long enough for Zekk to give the order to dock. He was tense as the shuttle approached, unsure of the reception Brakiss would give him.

Beside him, in the command cockpit, Tamith Kai seethed silently, her wine-dark lips pressed together in a cold line, but she said nothing. Zekk had lost not only the team of stormtroopers directly under his command in the treetop city, but also two of her greatest Nightsister allies. Both Vonnda Ra and Garowyn were presumed dead in the depths of Kashyyyk's jungles.

Though Zekk had not been with either Nightsister when they had died or disappeared, Tamith Kai blamed him for the debacle, as she blamed him for the death of her prime student Vilas. Tamith Tai resented his presence—though presumably she and Zekk both worked toward the ultimate victory of the Second Imperium. All other losses, he felt, should simply be considered the price of their ultimate triumph.

But Tamith Kai was not pleased with how the young man had handled himself on Kashyyyk. And so, during their return from the fateful mission, Zekk kept to himself, avoiding direct contact with the Nightsister.

He brought the assault ship in, sitting in the command chair while other Imperial pilots handled the controls, guiding the craft into the Shadow Academy's open docking bay. As they entered, he saw another armored shuttle—an impressive Imperial transport surrounded by deadly force fields—and wondered what had happened during his absence.

The battered assault craft, with its precious cargo of stolen computer components, settled into place with what sounded like a mechanical sigh of relief. "We have landed, Lord Zekk," the pilot said.

The tactical officer studied the controls. "The Shadow Academy's cloaking device has been reactivated. The station is once again undetectable by Rebel sensors."

The hatches opened, and the crew began filing out. Stormtroopers marched up from the Shadow Academy's interior to surround the battered shuttle, ready to unload the stolen cargo as soon as Zekk released it.

Tamith Kai stood beside him in the cockpit; with a flick of her shoulder, she tossed her spined black cape back. Her long-nailed fingers balled into fists as she struggled to contain the fury within her. The electric fire in her violet eyes boiled like lava.

Zekk closed his dark-ringed emerald eyes and drew a deep breath to focus his thoughts, center his concentration. He let her anger wash over his mind and drain away. His greatest concern was Master Brakiss and how he would face him. His teacher had such high hopes for him, and he might be even more displeased than Tamith Kai. Contemplating the probable disappointment of his mentor hurt Zekk more than any display of rage by the continually bothersome Nightsister from Dathomir.

Squaring his shoulders, he straightened his padded leather armor and adjusted his crimson-lined black cape. He tossed his long dark hair behind him and turned toward the assault craft's hatch, making himself an imposing figure, ominous and menacing. He had learned such posturing from observing Tamith Kai herself, and it amused him to think he could use her own techniques of intimidation against her.

With the tall Nightsister following him, Zekk strode down the ramp like a conquering hero. Inside his heart, though, dread grew.

The sculpture-handsome teacher stood at the edge of the airlock bay, watching the proceedings. As Zekk emerged, Brakiss glided forward with smooth, even footsteps. His silvery robes clung around him like whispers.

Zekk held his chin high, looking into the open, clear gaze of Brakiss. The master of the Shadow Academy folded his hands in front of him. "Young Zekk, my Darkest Knight, you have returned from your first mission. Report. Were you successful?"

Zekk swallowed hard and gave his straightforward account. "Unfortunately, Master Brakiss, our mission did not come off as smoothly as we had planned. During our battles at the fortified Wookiee facilities, we lost fourteen TIE fighters and bombers, as well as eleven ground assault troops.

"It is also my duty to report that we lost two of our Nightsister companions: Vonnda

Ra in the lower levels of the forest, and Garowyn, who was apparently murdered when she tried to reclaim our *Shadow Chaser*."

Brakiss showed no reaction and waited. Finally he said, "But the computer components—the guidance and tactical systems? Did you succeed in obtaining the vital resources the Second Imperium requires?"

Zekk flinched. "Yes, Master Brakiss. All of the computer equipment is stored inside this assault transport, ready for distribution to the Second Imperium."

Brakiss clapped his hands together. "Excellent! Then your mission was a success, with acceptable losses of personnel. Those other . . . *inconveniences* are insignificant in our overall conflict. You have achieved our most important goal."

Tamith Kai's eyes widened with anger, and her normally pale face flushed a blotchy red. "Master Brakiss!" she hissed. "Zekk also claims to have removed those Jedi brats. But although Vonnda Ra accompanied him to this confrontation, Zekk returned alone . . . claiming victory."

Zekk stood rigid. "The young Jedi Knights are no longer a problem," he said. "This I swear."

Tamith Kai obviously didn't believe him.

But Brakiss did, and that was all that counted.

Zekk didn't know how long he could keep up the charade. He had fallen to the dark side—and he had also protected his friends. The two seemed incompatible. Sooner or later, Brakiss would learn what he had done—and then Zekk would face an impossible choice. But, as always, no one else would make Zekk's choices for him . . . and no one else would face the consequences.

"The Second Imperium applauds your efforts, Zekk. The history of the galaxy will remember you as an instrumental fighter in our grand cause."

Zekk knew he should have felt better, prouder . . . but he could summon no emotion other than dread. And disappointment in himself. He was no longer sure of where his past decisions would lead him.

One of the stormtroopers standing in ranks within the hangar bay shifted uneasily. Zekk focused his attention on the burly trooper—instinctively identifying Norys. Qorl stood beside the bully, frowning in disapproval at his white-armored trainee. The leader of the Lost Ones still bore a chip on his shoulder, resulting in a perpetually surly attitude.

Suddenly, the air in the huge docking bay

shimmered. Zekk looked up as the other stormtroopers backed away. Beside him, Brakiss grew tense, almost fearful, but stood his ground against the projection.

An image formed in the air, a giant cowled head with yellow eyes and an age-ravaged face that emanated dark power. The visage of Emperor Palpatine was incredibly clear and focused, as if the transmission came from very close. Very close indeed.

"My subjects at the Shadow Academy," the Emperor's shuddering voice said, "my fellow fighters in the cause of the Second Imperium, I am pleased to learn of this successful mission! Through our various raids and by gathering the scattered remnants of my lost Imperial glory, we now have the might to move on to the next phase in our plan of conquest. The new hyperdrive cores and turbolaser batteries have already been installed in our secret battle fleet. I have commanded that the new computer components be incorporated immediately. We must strike again while the Rebels are still reeling."

Under the leather padding, Zekk felt a cold, damp shiver work its way down his back.

"It is our mission to remove the only real line of defense the Rebels have against us.

Brakiss, you promised me an invincible fighting force of Dark Jedi Knights. The time has come to make use of them.

"Together, as our primary campaign, we shall attack and destroy Luke Skywalker's Jedi academy. Those light side Jedi will be crushed to dust beneath our feet.

"I command you all to move out. Set the Shadow Academy forces in motion. We must transport our station to the jungle moon of Yavin 4 without delay. Once we have eliminated the new Jedi Knights, the galaxy will be ours for the taking."

Zekk stood stunned. Brakiss stared at the fading image of the Emperor in amazement. Then, as if a power switch had been flicked on, all of the stormtroopers sprang into motion.

The Shadow Academy rushed to prepare for its greatest battle.

22

IN THE AFTERMATH of the devastating attack on the Wookiee computer fabrication facility, Jaina knew they could not afford to wait. Too much was at risk—and right now.

While the New Republic forces sent a few nearby ships filled with a complement of engineers and soldiers to help in reparation activities, Jaina and Lowie worked tirelessly with Chewbacca to complete repairs to the *Shadow Chaser*. The tall Wookiee still limped on his sore leg, but his injuries had mostly healed, and he didn't let a little stiffness slow him down.

Inside the crowded power-supply bulkhead of the *Shadow Chaser*, Jaina, the smallest of the workers, crammed herself deep into the tightest spaces, hooking up power leads and disconnecting diagnostics. All the replacement parts had been ready even before the

Imperial attack on Kashyyyk, but now the sleek vessel needed to be reassembled.

"Power it up before I crawl back out of here," Jaina said. "All the circuits are grounded and shielded, but I want to make sure everything checks out before I fight my way into open air again."

Lowie grunted and flicked a power switch. He and Chewbacca simultaneously roared an affirmative.

Jaina heaved a sigh of relief. "Well, I'm glad the ship's functioning again," she said. "We have to get out of here and back to Yavin 4 before the attack comes. We need to be ready for the Shadow Academy." She swallowed. "We've all been training a long time for this."

Lowie roared in agreement, though he and Chewbacca and Sirra seemed somewhat saddened. Sirra growled a series of notes, and Em Teedee said, "Mistress Sirrakuk says that she will stay to help her people clean up and make repairs, but she understands that her brother Lowbacca must return to fight with the other Jedi. There are many Wookiees who can assist here on Kashyyyk, but there aren't many other Jedi Knights . . . and she is exceedingly proud that her brother is one of them."

Lowie rumbled his appreciation.

Em Teedee added, as an aside, "I do believe she's quite pleased with him."

Sirra patted her big brother on his hairy shoulder, then proudly ran one hand over her glossy new belt, woven from the strands of fiber she had harvested from the syren plant. Jaina knew that Sirra's personal opportunities were now wide open, possibilities for her life that had always been there . . . but that she would now be better able to take advantage of.

Jacen rushed aboard the *Shadow Chaser* carrying the small cage with his pet Ion and her babies. He cooed reassurances to the furry rodents.

Tenel Ka accompanied him, looking confident in her freshly polished reptilian armor. She had reworked all of her braids meticulously, brushing her hair out and plaiting it using the new one-handed technique Anakin Solo had developed for her. "We are prepared to depart," she said. "And we are ready to fight as true Jedi Knights."

Lowie roared with enthusiasm. Sirra embraced her big brother, and then each of the young Jedi Knights.

Chewbacca limped up the ramp and

strapped himself into the *Shadow Chaser*'s pilot seat. Lowie slid into the seat behind his uncle, flipping on the controls and powering up the various subsystems. The two Wookiees barked a preflight checklist back and forth.

Sirrakuk slipped back out of the sleek ship and stood watching as the craft prepared to depart. Within moments the *Shadow Chaser* rose up on its repulsorlifts, bearing its message of warning to Luke Skywalker and his Jedi academy.

"We've just sent the alert to Yavin 4, but now we have to go," Jaina told her brother. "Uncle Luke is back from his scouting mission with Dad—but the Jedi academy is still in danger."

"I've got a bad feeling about this," Jacen agreed.

He held the small cage in his lap, still whispering soothing words. Tenel Ka sat beside Jacen, eager to go. She brushed her fingers over the weapons at her belt, anticipating the fight to come.

Chewbacca yowled a brief order to prepare for acceleration, then the *Shadow Chaser* leaped skyward. A few minutes later, they catapulted into hyperspace and left Kashyyyk behind.

They raced back to Yavin 4 at full speed, knowing they had to prepare for the greatest challenge of their lives.

The Shadow Academy was coming.

At last, the final confrontation with the Shadow Academy . . .

Jedi Under Siege

The day of reckoning is at hand for the young Jedi Knights. The Shadow Academy—with its army of Dark Jedi and Imperial stormtroopers—has appeared in the sky over Yavin 4. And when a commando raid destroys the shield generator protecting the Jedi academy, there is only one option: to fight.

Now Jacen and Jaina, along with Luke Skywalker and their friends, must trust in the Force and do battle with their sworn enemies—the Dark Jedi Zekk, his master Brakiss, and the loathsome Nightsister Tamith Kai. Victory means a new legacy of Jedi coming of age. Defeat means a final cloak of darkness over the entire galaxy . . .

Turn the page for a special preview
of the next book in the
STAR WARS: YOUNG JEDI KNIGHTS series:
Jedi Under Siege
Coming in September from Boulevard Books!

In the uncertain pre-dawn light, Jaina watched her uncle, Luke Skywalker, maneuver the *Shadow Chaser* into the Jedi academy's hangar bay at the base of the Great Temple. Her father, Han Solo, and Chewbacca had not even stayed long enough to perform that chore when the young Jedi Knights returned from the Wookiee homeworld of Kashyyyk.

With the Shadow Academy on the move, they had no time to lose.

Jaina found it hard to believe that barely two days earlier Kashyyyk had been under attack by Imperial forces led by none other than her friend Zekk, now a Dark Jedi in service of the Second Imperium. When she'd confronted the dark-haired young man in the forest underlevels, he had warned her not to return to Yavin 4 because the Shadow Academy would attack soon.

Jaina had to believe the warning was a sign that Zekk still cared about her and her twin brother, Jacen.

She and her friends had been back on Yavin 4 for only a few minutes. None of them had gotten much sleep on the swift hyperspace flight back, but they all ran on adrenaline. Jaina felt as if she would explode if she couldn't *do* something right away. So many preparations to make, so much to plan.

Standing beside her near the entrance to the hangar bay, Jacen gave her a nudge. When she glanced at him, his brandy-brown eyes looked straight into hers. "Hey, it'll be *okay*," he said. "Uncle Luke will know what to do. He's been through plenty of Imperial attacks before."

"Sure, that makes me feel a lot better," she answered, not believing it for a minute.

As usual, Jacen resorted to one of his favorite techniques to get her mind off the battle that was sure to come. "Hey, want to hear a joke?"

"Yes Jacen," said Tenel Ka, striding up to join them. "I believe humor could be of some use now." The warrior girl from Dathomir glistened with perspiration from having spent the last ten minutes running "to stretch her muscles" to work off her own tension.

"Okay, Jacen. Fire away," Jaina said, pretending to brace herself for the worst.

Tenel Ka pushed back her long, reddish-gold braids with her one arm. Her left arm had been severed in a terrible accident during lightsaber training, and she refused to accept a synthetic replacement. She nodded to Jacen. "You may proceed with the joke."

"Okay, what time is it when an Imperial walker steps on your wrist-chronometer?" Jacen raised his eyebrows, waiting. "Time to get a new chronometer!"

After a heartbeat of dead silence, Tenel Ka nodded and said in a serious voice, "Thank you, Jacen. Your humor was quite . . . adequate."

The warrior girl never cracked a smile, but Jaina thought she detected a twinkle in her friend's cool gray eyes. Jaina was still groaning in mock agony when Luke and the young Wookiee Lowbacca climbed out of the *Shadow Chaser*.

Without a moment to lose, Jaina hurried over to them. Apparently Uncle Luke felt the same way—when Jacen and Tenel Ka trotted up behind her, the Jedi Master began to speak without preamble.

"It'll take the Second Imperium some time to install the new computer components they stole for their fleet," Luke said. "We may have a few days yet, but I don't want to take any chances. Lowie—Tionne and Raynar went out to the temple on the lake for a training exercise. I'd like you to take your T-23 and go bring them back here. We all need to work together."

Lowie roared an acknowledgment and sprinted for the small skyhopper his uncle Chewbacca had given him. From the clip at Lowie's waist the miniaturized translating droid, Em Teedee, said, "Why certainly, sir. It would be Master Lowbacca's great pleasure to be of service. Consider it done." Reprimanding the little droid for its embellishments with an absent growl, the young Wookiee climbed into the small T-23 and closed the canopy.

Luke turned to the warrior girl from Dathomir. "Tenel Ka, gather as many students as you can and give them a crash course in ground combat against terrorist attacks. I'm not sure what strategies the Shadow Academy will use, but I can't think of anyone better to teach them about assassins and commando tactics than you."

"Yeah, she was great against those Bartokk assassins on Hapes," Jacen said.

Tenel Ka surprised Jaina by blushing pink before she gave a curt nod and sped off on her assignment.

"What about Jacen and me, Uncle Luke?" Jaina asked, bursting with impatience. "What should we do? We want to help."

"Now that the *Millennium Falcon* is gone, we need to get the new shield generators back up and running to protect us from an aerial attack. Come with me."

The Jedi academy's new defensive shield generators were controlled from the Comm Center. Han Solo had recently brought the components from Coruscant as a stop-gap measure while the New Republic scrambled to assemble a major defense against the impending Imperial attack.

"Hey, should I send a message to Mom?" Jacen asked, sitting down at one of the consoles.

"Not until we know more," Luke answered. "Your dad and Chewie were going to contact her and explain everything once they were under way. Leia has her hands full mustering whatever troops she can spare to station here as permanent protectors for the Jedi academy. Meanwhile, *we've* got to do everything we can to guard it ourselves.

"Meanwhile, Jacen, monitor all the communications bands. See if you can pick up any signals, especially ones that might be Imperial codes. Jaina, let's get those shield generators powered up and running. The primary equipment is across the river out in the jungle, but you can operate them remotely from here."

"Already on it, Uncle Luke." Jaina grinned at him from the control station. "Shields are up and at full strength. Guess I should run a complete readiness check, though, just to make sure there are no gaps in our defenses."

Jacen put on a headset and began scanning through the various comm frequencies. No sooner had he begun than a loud crackle erupted from the earpiece, followed by a familiar voice.

". . . requesting permission for landing and all that usual stuff. Here I come. *Lightning Rod* out."

"Hey, wait!" Jacen said into the voice pickup, on the verge of panic. "You can't do that—I mean, we have to drop our shields first. Give me a minute, Peckhum."

"Shields? What shields?" the old spacer's voice came back. "Me and the *Lightning Rod* been doin' the supply run to Yavin 4 for years now. Never had to worry about shields before."

"We'll meet you down at the landing pad and explain everything," Jacen said. "Hang on a minute."

"Am I going to need a code to get in?" Peckhum asked. "No one gave me any codes before I left Coruscant. Nobody told me about any shields."

Jacen looked up at Luke. "It's old Peckhum in the *Lightning Rod*," he said. "Does he need a code to get in?"

Luke shook his head and motioned for Jaina to drop the shields. Jaina bent over the control console, her lower lip caught between her teeth. After a minute she said, "There, that ought to do it. Shields lowered again."

For some reason, now that the shields were down Jacen felt a cold tingle of vulnerability run up the back of his neck. "Okay, Peckhum," he said, "you're clear to land. But make it quick, so we can power up again."

When the old spacer stepped out of his battered supply shuttle, he looked the same as every other time Jacen had seen him: pale skin, long lanky hair, grizzled cheeks, and rumpled flight suit.

"Come on, Peckhum," Jacen said. "I'll help you get the supplies inside. We need to hurry, before the Imperials get here."

"Imperials?" The spacer scratched his head. "Is that why you've got energy shields up? Are we under attack?"

"It's okay," Jacen said, impatient to get the *Lightning Rod* unloaded. "The shields are back up. You just can't see them."

The old spacer craned his neck to stare up into the misty white sky of the jungle moon. "And the attack?"

"Well, we heard a rumor—a pretty good one." He hesitated. "From Zekk. He's the one who led the raid on the computer fabrication facility on Kashyyyk—and he warned Jaina that the Shadow Academy is on its way."

Old Peckhum looked at Jacen in alarm. Young Zekk had been like a son to him; they had lived together in the lower city levels on Coruscant . . . until Zekk had been kidnapped by the Shadow Academy.

As a familiar cold tingle crept up the back of Jacen's neck, Peckhum whispered, "Too late." He pointed to the sky. "They're already here."